Complications

"Life's simple for you, isn't it?" Matt asked.

"No, life has never been simple for me," Jessie replied. "You're not simple. But we mean something to each other, though I don't know for sure what. And it's going to be hard to keep ignoring it, don't you think?"

"Yeah," he said finally. "It's going to be hard to ignore it. But sometimes the harder way's the better. In the end, I mean."

"You're pontificating, Professor, and not making a lot of sense."

Jessie could see the struggle in Matt's eyes. She started to shiver and knew then she'd better get out of the car fast. She needed a hot bath—or Matt's arms—to warm her body. And something inside her told her the hot bath would be easier to deal with. At least for tonight.

Dear Reader:

As you can see, Silhouette Desire has a bold new cover design that we're all excited about. But while the overall look is new, two things remain the same. First, we've kept our eye-catching red border. You can be sure to always spot Silhouette Desires on the shelves! Second, between these new covers are the high-quality love stories that you've come to expect.

In addition, the MAN OF THE MONTH program continues with Mr. September, who comes from the pen of Dixie Browning. Clement Cornelius Barto is a unique hero who is sure to charm you with his unusual ways. But make no mistake, it's not just *Beginner's Luck* that makes him such a winner.

October brings you a man who's double the fun, because not only is Jody Branigan an exciting hero, he's also one of Leslie Davis Guccione's Branigan brothers. Look for his story in *Branigan's Touch*.

We at Silhouette have been happy to hear how much you've all enjoyed the Year of the Man. The responses we've received about the special covers—and to each and every one of our heroes—has been enthusiastic. Remember, there are more men ahead in 1989—don't let any of them get away!

Yours,

Lucia Macro
Senior Editor

SALLY GOLDENBAUM

ONCE IN LOVE WITH JESSIE

SILHOUETTE *Desire*

Published by Silhouette Books New York

America's Publisher of Contemporary Romance

 SILHOUETTE BOOKS
300 East 42nd St., New York, N.Y. 10017

ISBN: 0-373-05520-X

First Silhouette Books printing September 1989

All the characters in this book are fictitious. Any
resemblance to actual persons, living or dead, is
purely coincidental.

Printed in the U.S.A.

Silhouette Desire

Honeymoon Hotel #423
Chantilly Lace #460
Once in Love with Jessie #520

SALLY GOLDENBAUM

Born in Wisconsin, Sally now lives in Missouri, where she has been successfully writing contemporary romance novels for the past five years, as well as teaching at the high school and college levels. Married for almost twenty years, Sally holds a master's degree in philosophy and has worked both as a textbook writer and as a public relations writer for public television.

One

She was having a staredown with a bagel.

At least that's what it looked like from where Matt Ridgefield stood on the corner of Sixth Avenue and Jones. He frowned, shoved his hands into the pockets of his suit pants and began to walk away. But something stopped him, one of those odd nudges in life that you wondered about for years, and he turned to look again.

The woman stood directly in front of the deli on Jones Avenue. She took one step toward the large plate-glass window, one step backward, then moved forward again, her nose nearly rubbing the surface this time.

She reminded Matt of a dancer doing warm-ups, and without realizing he was doing so, he walked closer.

"This is cruel and inhuman punishment," the dark-haired woman murmured as she stared through the glass at the aproned baker on the other side.

The round baker was molding soft dough into dough-nut-shaped pieces and dropping them into a vat of boiling water. As soon as he finished that, he opened an oven door and pulled out a giant tray of finished bagels—hot, perfectly shaped golden circles that glistened like suntanned skin.

"Damn!" she said, one finger tapping irritably at the window and leaving smudged ovals on the glass.

Standing next to her now, Matt straightened his slightly crooked tie and looked at her through dark-rimmed glasses. "You're leaving marks on the window," he said matter-of-factly.

She looked up at him. "I'd like to leave more than that."

"Why?" Matt asked. "Overpriced? Bad dough?"

"Oh, no, never." She sighed. "It's because making bagels like that—by the window, I mean, where everybody can watch—is awful. Almost immoral." She edged her way toward the shop door. Then as if struck by an important thought, she stopped short and looked again at Matt, who was still standing in front of the window. "I'm on a diet, you see." Her dark brows arched. "I've lost five pounds. I don't need this." She gave a small shrug, half smiled at Matt and went inside. He followed.

The man behind the counter greeted the woman by her first name and she asked him about his daughter's newborn girl. Then she ordered a coffee, two poppy seed bagels with cream cheese and looked longingly through the case at the pickles: huge, fat, juicy, kosher dills. "Hmm," she moaned.

"High salt content," said Matt at her elbow.

She looked up at the horn-rimmed glasses. "Don't tell me about salt content. As long as I'm ruining my day, I might as well have high blood pressure along with fat."

"But pickles for breakfast?" Matt said.

"Maybe I'm pregnant."

He looked down at the close-fitting jeans and soft cotton shirt she wore, and smiled with a slight apology attached. "I'm butting in, aren't I?"

Jessie Sager examined the man closely. He wore a three-piece suit and looked, not exactly uncomfortable, but as if he'd much rather be in jeans and a work shirt. His smile wasn't enormous, but he looked friendly enough. "The way I see it," Jessie said after a moment of thought, "is that we don't butt into each other's lives enough. We'd have less wars if we cared more about our neighbor's screwy breakfast habits." And then she laughed.

It was a deep, clear and ringing laugh that lit her face so beautifully that Matt smiled.

"Maybe so," Matt murmured, but his thoughts were on the tiny green flecks that danced in her brown eyes and caught the sunlight, rather than his meaningless words.

Jessie pointed to the one empty table left in the crowded shop. "Looks like there's only one table left. Shall we share it and explore each other's nutsy breakfast habits? What are you having, by the way?"

She caught him off guard. "Just coffee."

"In Bagels, Bialys and Blintzes? Immoral."

"I already ate," he said. "I need to go."

"It's hard to walk and drink coffee. You'll spill it on that great-looking suit. Come on and sit for ten minutes." She turned and headed for the table without waiting for an answer.

Matt's eyes followed her. He checked his watch. As usual, he was early. He had plenty of time before the meeting began.

"Come on." She was calling to him from the green Formica-topped table against the wall.

Matt frowned. Then he turned back, ordered a cup of decaffeinated coffee and carried it carefully to where she sat. He decided not to question his uncharacteristic behavior and instead simply walked toward the woman with expressive eyes, as if it were something he did every day. Besides, he could use another cup of coffee.

After she had arranged her plastic plate of food in front of her, she looked up at him and smiled. "Hi," she said. "I'm Jessie Sager."

"Matt Ridgefield," he replied.

Jessie looked at him more carefully now. He was handsome in an odd sort of way, even though he didn't smile much. But when he *did* manage a half smile, his jawline softened, which gave him a slightly boyish look. He had intelligent, brooding blue eyes behind the glasses and she guessed he was in his late thirties, although when he gave that half grin, ten of those years disappeared. She didn't think she'd ever seen him around the deli before.

"Do you come here often?" she asked.

"No," Matt answered. "I was just passing by on my way to a meeting. When I heard you swearing at the window, I noticed you, and then I noticed the coffee sign."

Jessie laughed. "Sorry about the swearing. It's just that the world conspires against me sometimes, and I need to let out a little hostility. Normally I'm a very pleasant person."

"I'm sure you are."

"The day started out in an awkward way and I haven't had a chance to rise above it—but I will."

"Oh?" Matt said. He looked around, slightly uncomfortable in her presence. She talked so much and seemed to act as if they had known each other a long time. There was an intimacy about the whole scene that made him shove his chair back an inch.

Her head nodding, Jessie swallowed a bite of bagel. "My shower was broken, so I used my neighbor's. Except he forgot to tell his dog, and Shakespeare took off with my clothes. Shakespeare is the dog, not my friend. Anyway, I had a towel so it was okay. But unpleasant, you know?"

Matt nodded. "And chilly I suppose," he said. "I hate it when that happens."

Jessie couldn't tell whether he was kidding or not, but then she checked his eyes and she laughed. He *was* kidding. Good. "Right," she said. "Enough about starting the day with Shakespeare. Tell me about you, Matt Ridgefield, and what brings you to Bagels, Bialys and Blintzes."

Matt took a drink of coffee and carefully set his cup down as if the action took thought. Then he tilted his head to one side and looked at Jessie. "You do, I guess. Like I said, I saw you outside."

Jessie's eyes widened. "You didn't come in here to eat?"

"No. Just for coffee."

"You followed me?" He certainly didn't look like a masher, but Jessie was a little unsettled nevertheless. She never expected an attempted pickup in the bagel shop. And certainly not at this hour of the morning by a man who reminded her a little of the star of her favorite show, *The Rockford Files*. "Why did you follow me?"

Matt tried to shrug off her question because he didn't really have an answer. He hadn't actually followed her. In fact, to anyone who knew him, the idea would be considered laughable. The reverse, women following him, was far more likely. He sipped his coffee and shrugged. "Maybe it was the bagels, or the combination."

Jessie looked at him intently. No, this man wasn't a masher. And who was she to question his motives? She talked to strangers all the time. "Well, it's nice having company. And you seem safe enough."

Matt half smiled.

"Do you work around here?" Jessie asked.

"No. I work across town. How about you?"

"I work nearby."

"Do you want another bagel?"

She looked down at her plate. Except for a few dollops of cream cheese that had oozed out, it was empty. She groaned. "Do you know how many calories are in all this?"

"No."

"Me, neither. It's too depressing to think about. No, I can't have another bagel, but thank you. You've been a wonderful breakfast companion. And now I have to get to work, or they'll send out the marines."

"Where do you work?"

Her face fell. For a moment she looked so sad that Matt thought she was going to cry. But then her smile reappeared, pushing away the emotion that had completely shrouded her face seconds before. Amazing, Matt thought. The emotion was real, he didn't doubt it for a moment; what amazed him was the strength she had to compartmentalize things so that the emotion was lassoed and put back in its place nearly as quickly as it had surfaced.

"I write copy for a little neighborhood newspaper. Our office is on Harrison Street. But it's a very tender spot, because I've been fired."

Matt leaned forward. "Fired?" Why would any sane person fire this woman?

"Yep." Jessie finished the last drops of her coffee and set the cup on her plate. Sighing softly, she dug her fingers into the Styrofoam cup. "And I liked this job, Matt. Especially the people I worked with. We *all* lost our jobs.

The paper's folding because there aren't enough merchants to support it.''

"That's too bad," Matt said. He needed to leave, to get on with his day. This was silly, sitting here with a stranger and listening to her problems. But his legs wouldn't move.

"It's not exactly a new experience for me," Jessie said. "I seem to pick jobs with limited life spans. My résumé is nearly as long as the Great Wall of China."

"What will you do?"

"Well, we're winding things up at the paper, so I still have a place to hang my hat for a couple of weeks. Then it's off to see Janet at Acme Employment Agency, I guess. Or maybe something will come up in the meantime." She shrugged.

"What kind of job do you want?" Matt focused on her problem, which was something he was used to and found easier to deal with than the peculiar overtones of Jessie's presence. Students had problems all the time—money problems, job problems, an endless parade.

"I want a job that makes a lot of money." Jessie laughed and Matt noticed again how the flecks in her eyes danced. "Do I sound mercenary?"

Matt shrugged. "Practical, maybe."

"That's it," she said. "Practical Jess. What I really want to do is win the lottery. That would solve a whole wheelbarrow full of problems. Now how's that for practical?"

"Some people do I guess."

"But not Jessie. I'm not lucky. Not like that. But something will turn up." She paused, and when she spoke again her eyes were twinkling. "Sometimes my friends read my résumé at parties instead of playing Trivial Pursuit. There ought to be something there I can draw on."

Matt watched her carefully, trying to listen to her conversation. He was finding it more and more difficult because everything else about her assaulted his senses in a very unexpected way.

She was standing up now, the crumpled mass that remained of her breakfast held in her hands and a large woven purse slung over one shoulder.

"You have to get to work?" he asked, pushing back his chair.

She nodded. "I should. There are a lot of winding-up things to do." Her large brown eyes were focused on his face. "But this was nice, having someone to talk to. And you're nice, too. You're a good listener, Matt Ridgefield."

Before Matt could stand, she was already moving away.

"No, wait," he said, straightening so abruptly that his empty cup fell over.

Jessie turned around at the urgency in his voice.

"I thought of a job you might be interested in."

Jessie walked back to the table. "Oh?"

"It occurred to me just this instant."

Jessie took a seat and smiled at him. "I'm all ears. I guess my stuffed files and the mess on my desk can wait a little longer to be cleaned out and banished to the trash can."

Matt stood for a minute looking at her. He should have thought of it sooner. She'd be perfect for the job. And this whole crazy incident would be back in perspective.

"Well, tell me about this job, Matt. Will it make me rich?"

"Why is that so important to you, Jessie?" Matt frowned and sat down at the table.

"Being rich?"

"Yes."

Jessie fiddled with the strap of her purse. "Well, it's a long, boring story, Matt. But really it's not wanting to be rich as much as it's wanting not to have to worry about money. That's such a waste of good energy. When you don't have enough money for some important things, you worry about it. So that's one reason I'd like to be moneyed." She paused. "Moneyed. That's a much better word than rich, don't you think?"

"This deal might make you moneyed for a while," he said. "It's a modeling job."

Jessie laughed. It was deep and throaty and filled the small deli. She tucked her head down to her chest and swallowed the last of her laughter, pulling together a semiserious expression. "Matt, if you're trying to pick me up, that's as old as the dust under my bed. Let's be original about this. A model! I'm five foot five, didn't you see?" She started to stand and a flurry of papers fell from her purse to the floor. Jessie ignored them. "And look!" She pointed to her well-shaped breasts. "My mother's genes. All her sisters were like this, too. Models are flat and willowy, not full of more curves than San Francisco's Lombard Street."

She stopped for breath and noticed the beginnings of laughter coming from Matt's eyes. "What's so funny?"

Matt shook his head. "You. You're funny, Jessie Sager. And nice to be with. And I think you might fit this job perfectly. Maybe *model* isn't the right word."

"You meant to say writer, right? Okay, we'll talk."

Matt sat back in the chair. It had occurred to him suddenly that he found being in Jessie's presence, with all her energy and life, strangely peaceful. The contradiction was curious but he pushed it aside to pursue the matter at hand—employing Jessie. "What I'm talking about is a special type of modeling job. I have a friend with a new

company called Dining Delux, and they need some people
for an advertising campaign. Next-door types, ordinary
people—"

"Ordinary?" Jessie interrupted. "You think I'm ordinary?"

Her gentle teasing was like a soft summer breeze.
"Sorry, that was a terrible choice of words. You're not
ordinary, no. But you're not model-like, either—"

"That's what I was saying."

"But you have a sort of charm. I'd bet you could sell air
conditioners to Eskimos."

"How much does that pay?" He half smiled again.
Jessie found she was looking forward to the slight grins.

"Seriously," Matt said. "You really might be interested in this. Something's better than nothing, right?"

Jessie couldn't argue or tease on that one. She forked her
fingers through her thick black hair. She suddenly felt naked. It was slowly dawning on her that Matt was earnest.
And that he was probably, at this very moment, examining her un-model-like characteristics carefully and precisely. But this was all craziness. She, Jessica Esther Sager,
a model?

"Matt," she said slowly, "I think you're nice. And even
though I thought at first you were pulling my leg—my
short legs, as you might have noticed—I believe you now.
So now you have to believe me. I'm not the model type,
ordinary or not, honest. I used to itch so badly when my
mother hemmed my dresses that she'd have my little sister
stay close by to scratch me. I can't stand still very long."

Matt's gaze remained steady. He shrugged slightly. "It's
your choice. It's a simple television ad. People will audition, they'll pick a few, the chosen will get a hefty hunk of
money for a few days' easy work, and those who don't
make it will go on to other things. No big deal."

"Nothing ventured, nothing gained."

"Yeah. But it's up to you. I don't mean to pressure you. It just came to me as you were leaving that you might like a shot at it."

Jessie's thoughts flitted between a stack of unpaid bills on her desk at home and a "hefty hunk of money." "You're quite serious about all this, aren't you?"

It wasn't really a question so Matt didn't bother to answer. Jessie went on, "Tell me more about it."

"You show up, follow directions, diaper a baby, get into a car, that sort of thing. They need a person who looks as if she could do anything—work, play, have kids."

"I fit that, I guess," Jessie said. "Except for the kids. I mean, I love kids. I work with them over at the orphanage and I'm going to have a houseful someday, but I haven't actually *done* that yet."

"Well, that's okay," Matt assured her. She seemed interested now, so he continued. "It'll be simple. You do what they say, and then smile like you absolutely couldn't get through your day without the product."

"What's the product?"

"It's a line of frozen, prepared foods."

Jessie laughed. And then just as quickly, her face grew serious. "I don't know, Matt. What if I didn't like it? The food, I mean?"

Matt looked at her carefully. She was absolutely serious. "Oh, well, I think you will. If not, I guess you could fake it."

"No. No, I couldn't do that." She scowled and smoothed a napkin on the table.

Matt noticed she was nibbling on her bottom lip, thinking.

"But I do like most food," she said finally. "I'm not really a finicky eater."

"The job pays well," Matt added.

She laughed again and looked up at him. "You talk my language. Oh, what the hey, sure. I'll give it a try. If nothing else, it's a new category to add to my résumé."

Matt nodded.

"So what's first?"

Matt pulled a piece of paper out of his pocket. He scribbled down an address. "This is where they're auditioning. Be there Monday afternoon. There'll be other people there, too."

"It'll be fun," she said, her voice falling a little at the end.

"That's the spirit." Matt reached over and tucked the piece of paper into the pocket of her blouse.

Jessie looked at him, startled. It felt unexpectedly good, his large hand accidentally brushing her breast like that. And he smelled good, an odd mixture of pipe tobacco and the outdoors. She touched his arm. "Will you be there Monday?"

It occurred to Jessie somewhere between enjoying the light heat of his touch and listening to his words, that she didn't even know this man, what he did, what he was all about. And the oddest thing was that it didn't really matter a whole lot. He felt like a friend. She hoped he'd be there Monday.

Matt wrinkled his brow for a moment, as if mentally reading a calendar, sorting through dates and times. "Monday," he said. "I don't know. If I can, I'll come and cheer you on."

"But will you buy a frozen dinner, eh?" she joked as they stood up to go, and then she impulsively wrapped her arms around him in a quick hug and kissed him on the cheek. "Thanks, Matt."

Much later that day, when he finally put away the last of the students' papers and stepped onto the small patio outside his apartment for a late-night smoke, Matt couldn't remember much about their conversation—what he'd said, what she'd answered. But what he could remember, and what stayed with him through the quiet weekend, was the gentle press of Jessie Sager's lips on his cheek.

Two

___

Jessie walked carefully across the bedroom rug in her fourth-floor apartment, her arms stretched out to each side and a thick dictionary balanced precariously on top of her head. She caught her image in the oblong mirror on the wall and grimaced.

"This is a mistake," she moaned. "A major joke, you hear? I'm *not* a model."

Only the gurgle of her coffeepot and the crash of the book as it hit the floor answered the lament.

Jessie sighed. She glanced at the clock on the wall and dropped her arms. "Okay. So it's time. So I'll go. It'll be okay. I've done crazier things for jobs." But as she grabbed her sweater from a brass hook near the door, she was hard-pressed to think of any.

No, there was no precedent for this, and as she walked out of the apartment and huffed down the stairs, she wondered briefly just when she'd had the slight lapse of

sanity that made her agree to this. The only thing she knew
for sure was that it had something to do with Matt Ridgefield's eyes.

Matt stood at the fence and looked out over the fields as
far as his gaze would take him. From this spot he could see
for miles—fifteen or more he had decided one clear day—
and the changing terrain never ceased to work its magic on
him. Hills, valleys, woods and just a hint of the small
country town beyond the rolling pastures—they were all
there for him. His solitary world.

The autumn sunshine beat down on his bare back and
beneath the blanket of heat he stretched like a contented,
lazy cat. Life was okay out here on his land. Life was good.

He flung his shirt over his shoulder and turned from the
fence. As trite as it was, Matt thought, out here it was true:
all was right with the world, or at least as right as it could
get. His spacious house was just visible in the distance, a
quarter of a mile or so away beyond a small turn in the
woods. Matt headed back toward it, his head filled with
nothing, just the way he wanted it to be after a long weekend alone. He wasn't sure when she came into his
thoughts—some moment while he was striding across the
back lawns and before he reached the house. It had happened several times over the weekend—he had thought of
her. He'd be fixing a fence or walking alone at night along
the south edge of the property where you could almost
touch the moon, and she'd come to him, her eyes bright
with laughter, her husky voice teasing, and that careless
sensuality of hers wreaking a kind of havoc within him. He
didn't know what it was about Jessie Sager, but she wasn't
leaving him alone. She kept coming back, squeezing into
his thoughts, intruding on his sought-out solitude. And it
was a strange situation for Matt because women didn't

encroach on his private life unless he dictated it, and they *never* intruded on his life at Applewood. Applewood was his haven, the one place he could be completely himself, and in the ten years he'd owned the country estate, Matt had never once brought a woman there.

He glanced down at his wristwatch and noticed it was nearly noon. Noon of Jessie's audition day. That fact had occurred to him hours before when he had consciously made the decision not to show up. Jessie was an independent woman and she'd do just fine without a cheering section. Besides, as hard as he tried, he couldn't keep Jessie in her proper place in his mind. She refused to stay in the student category, the *young*-woman-met-accidentally-who-needed-help category; instead, without inhibition or reason, she jumped right over into other places where she had no right to be. And even though it was simply mental gymnastics at this point, Matt decided he didn't want to fool around with it.

So he'd stay away today, enjoy the extra few hours at the farm before going in for his late-afternoon class. He'd let the thoughts of Jessie fade away until they were obscure bits of nothing, faded memories of an interesting woman who'd walked in and out of his life in a day.

He took a cold shower, which felt good, and later Matt sat at the kitchen table praising his good sense. He settled back with a cup of coffee and a musty, thick edition of Plato's *Republic*. Just outside the window birds sang and in the distance he could hear the comfortable, pleasant sounds of horses neighing. Everything was as it should be.

But he couldn't concentrate.

Finally Matt closed the book, stood and walked across the kitchen. He looked out across the fields, but he didn't see the woods. He saw Jessie Sager. Matt scowled and shook his head. And then he closed the windows, threw his briefcase in the car and headed toward town.

"All right now, folks, we're going to give directions to everyone at the same time, then tape you individually. Don't worry about mistakes. We just want to see how you look on videotape for now. We'll do some voice tapes later on."

The man giving the directions looked like Arnold Schwarzenegger, Jessie thought, and the thought kept her spirit intact. Arnold Schwarzenegger directing a TV dinner spot. Would he strip to the waist and leap in with his tightly coiled muscles, balancing an aromatic dinner in his mighty palm? She held fast to the image.

A group of twenty or so people were sitting on folding chairs in a huge barn of a room. Several cameras fastened to tripods stood in front of them. Jessie sat in the last row. In one corner of the room there were some props: a bed, an easy chair, a microwave oven, a doll.

Jessie was nervous, but her own fear lessened when she looked at the thin woman sitting next to her. She had brown hair pulled back over her ears and she was looking straight ahead while tapping fiercely on her knee. It was red from the stern thumping of her fingers. Jessie breathed deeply. She wasn't *that* nervous. She'd be okay.

The director asked for quiet, and Jessie pressed her hand over her heart.

The first person called was a man who seemed to be somewhere between thirty and forty. He had a nice, familiar kind of face, Jess thought. Like Mr. Rogers. The Arnold look-alike pointed to some taped strips on the floor and told the man to stay within those marks. Then he walked over to a chair, sat down and told the man to act like a person who had just got home from a grueling day of fighting courtroom battles and was hungry as hell.

Jessie watched as the man hooked his index finger over the knot on his tie, tugged it loose and walked slowly across the room toward a chair. When he finally settled his weary body down into the cushion, it was all Jess could do to keep herself from bringing him slippers. He's good, she thought. Real good. The man began to speak then, in low, husbandlike tones, about how good it was to be home and what was that wonderful smell coming from the kitchen?

Matt Ridgefield hadn't told her she'd have to act for this! If he had, she would have told him what happened when she had to give her high school valedictorian speech. And she had never told *anyone* that. It was humiliation enough that the whole class of Cincinnati's Fairmont High School had struggled with each breath as Jessie stood and said: "Good...Good...Good...Good..." over and over and over again, until finally kind Principal Adams whispered loudly, "Good evening to you, Jessica." She had turned and smiled at him, relieved that someone understood. Then she had walked gratefully back to her seat with the principal and entire audience staring openmouthed at the shortest commencement speech on record at old FHS. She had vowed then never to speak in a public place with more than five people listening.

She took a deep breath. Maybe it was just the man who had to act.

When the thin woman was called up Jessie began to forget about herself and took on the woman's nervousness. She was ready to resume the symphony tapping on her own knee if it would help the lady. She looked so nervous Jessie was afraid she wouldn't make it to the front of the room. But when the lights were turned on and the woman swiveled and smiled out at the round camera lens,

Jessie had to blink hard. It *couldn't* be the same person. This new woman floated across the makeshift stage like Vanna White, smiling at imaginary dogs and kids, tucking sheets beneath mattresses so realistically that Jessie could smell the bleach.

Ohhh, Jessie groaned silently as she slid down lower on the chair. This *was* a mistake, no matter what Matt said. *Matt.* The thought made her turn around. She strained her neck to find the tall figure who had gotten her into this mess. He was nowhere to be seen. There was a nice, ordinary-looking man in a suit standing near the door. He seemed to have some authority and Jessie guessed maybe he was Matt's connection in all this. It was just as well Matt himself had decided not to show. That way she didn't know *anyone* here, and she'd never see any of them again, so what did it matter what happened?

"Sager? Anyone here named Sager?" The voice was loud and commanding and sliced through Jessie like a samurai's sword. Her heart stopped.

"Sager? Last call."

Again the voice assaulted her. Jessie looked around. No one was moving. Slowly she stood and walked to the front of the room.

"So there you are!" said the man. It was Arnold Schwarzenegger again.

"Okay. You look like the perfect young mother, and career woman. Right?"

Jessie didn't know if she was supposed to answer that. She decided on a slight nod of the head.

"Okay. It's morning, Ms. Sager. You're rushing around. Can't find your keys. Baby's crying. Then we'll do after work. Tired. Hard day. Forgot to thaw anything. Husband's coming home soon. Baby's still crying."

Poor thing, Jessie thought. Maybe he has the flu. Or worse, a pin stuck in him. She tried hard to concentrate.

"Questions?"

Jessie shook her head.

"Okay, let's see what you can do."

Jessie took a deep, calming breath. Then she began to walk across the stage. What had he said? Oh, she was rushed. Right. Jessie began to walk faster, back and forth. And then she remembered the baby. She had seen a doll on a desk. Quickly she traversed the stage again and grabbed the doll. It slipped. Not a great start, she thought, but the doll seemed all right. She bent over, grabbed it by the foot and swung it up easily. Okay. Rushed. Baby. Now keys.

Jessie spun around and moved across the stage, looking beneath the table and behind the chair, the doll dangling from her arm. She lost her keys sometimes and they always seemed to appear in unlikely places, like in the keyhole. But there wasn't a door. Maybe she should be clever. Find them in her shoe or behind her ear. She looked at the oven. Aha! With the baby tucked neatly under her arm, she headed for the stove.

In the back of the room there was a slight stir while someone came in. Matt walked over and stood next to Stan Jenkins. He'd dumped his stuff at his condominium near the campus, changed into his teaching clothes and then almost not come. But the dark-haired beauty wouldn't leave his thoughts alone. So he'd come. To exorcise his thoughts, he told himself.

"Don't tell me. Let me guess," Stan said quietly. "This is the friend you called me about."

Matt had called before leaving for the farm on Friday to let Stan know he was sending someone over for the auditions. He had assured Stan she wouldn't expect preferential treatment and Stan had assured him she wouldn't get it.

Matt couldn't answer Stan for a minute. He was watching Jessie try to open the oven door with the baby stuck beneath her arm. The doll's fat rubber legs stuck out in a victory sign next to Jessie's hip. He shook his head. "Interesting."

"Yep, and as lovely and bewitching as all get out. Too bad John Candy or Chevy Chase aren't around to play opposite her."

"Just a little stage jitters. Easy to fix," said Matt, his eyes glued to Jessie's shapely backside.

"Right. Sure. And she might sell some dinners, too, once we resuscitate the baby she dropped and do a little physical therapy on the consumers' necks that have been injured watching her crisscross the stage."

Matt looked at Stan to see if he was kidding. When he saw that his friend wasn't, he looked back at Jessie. She was hunched over now, pulling strenuously on the oven door. Just as Matt felt an incredible urge to go help her, the oven door flew open and Jessie sailed back across the floor on her nicely shaped rump. The baby landed in the oven.

Matt groaned and the roomful of people held back choked laughter.

The director stared, not knowing whether to scold her, hug her, or cry.

But before anyone could make a move, Jessie stood and looked over at the large, burly director. Her face was wet with perspiration, but the corners of her lips were lifted in a playful smile. "Okay, Hansel," she said. "You're next."

The group burst into laughter and Jessie gave a quick grateful nod. Then she headed for the door.

Matt strode over to her side.

Jessie looked up at him, a heated blush covering her face and neck. She felt wet all over and her hair was damp and clung to her cheeks in small dark curls.

"No," she said before he could speak. "I don't exactly blame you, Matt, but you *will* spend the rest of your life in reparation for getting me into this. And I want the guilt to go with you *everywhere*—work, home, to the sacred depths of your bedroom." She strung out the word *bedroom* until they reached the elevator.

When the doors opened, Matt followed her in.

"Well," Jessie said, her fingers curling into tight fists. She pressed them onto her hips and glared at him. "What do you have to say for yourself, sir?"

"How about a cup of coffee?" Matt grinned. He wasn't sure yet how she felt about what had happened, but he was sorry he had gotten her into it. He hadn't given her an inch to back out, but had railroaded her. He shoved his hands in his pockets and looked into her huge brown eyes. "What do you say to that?"

"Only if food goes along with it," Jessie grumbled.

Matt breathed easier.

When they were finally settled in the back booth of a coffee shop down the street, Matt decided to chance a smile. It grew broader as images of Jessie's curvaceous body sailing across the room filled his head. And when he remembered her final comment, he allowed a short laugh.

"The man laughs," Jessie said. "My career as a star ends in less than eight minutes—*and* on my tush!—and you laugh."

"Nope, you're wrong. Your career as a star will never end. And your young tush is lovely."

Jessie smiled. "Was that man, that Mr. Jenkins, your friend?" she asked.

"I think he probably still is. He thought you were charming. Bewitching, I think he said."

Jessie grimaced. "So have you seen any jobs for court jesters lately?" Then her expression grew sober. "It's nice to make people smile, Matt, but it doesn't buy bagels."

Matt grew serious along with her. His brows drew together. "I know. And I'm sorry for getting you into that. I didn't know—"

"What? That I was a bumpkin on stage?" She shrugged her shoulders and grinned. "What's to know? It's okay, Matt."

"I feel responsible. Maybe I can—"

Jessie stopped his words with her hands. "No. You're a nice man, Matt. I've certainly been without work before and flubbed interviews, but I've *never* taken handouts or considered others responsible. And it isn't your fault you're a lousy talent scout." She smiled as if to offer him some comfort.

"Hey, wait a minute, young woman," Matt said.

Jess noticed that when Matt talked seriously his head nodded slightly forward. It was a strangely boyish movement and she'd remember it whenever she thought about this nice man who had dropped into her life unexpectedly and tried to help her. Even though he'd failed miserably, she'd think of him fondly.

Matt went on. "I wasn't going to offer you a handout. I just thought I might be able to help. What kind of job do you want?"

"Writing, I guess, although the pay is miserable." The waitress set down a plate of hash browns and eggs in front of each of them and Jessie paused until the waitress walked away. "I don't know, Matt. Maybe I need some direction. Maybe someone new like you could put a fresh perspective on my life."

She looked at him so trustingly that Matt felt a tight squeeze around his heart. "Sure. I could try. I sometimes explore job markets for my kids."

Jessie's forkful of eggs stopped midair. Her eyes were as wide as saucers. "You help your who with what?"

"Kids, jobs." Matt shifted in his seat. Why was that so strange? And then it dawned on him. They didn't know anything about each other, basic facts that friends took for granted. It was strange, because it belied the feeling that was growing inside him about Jessie Sager. In there, he knew her. It was a feeling he had never had before. "Sorry," he said. "I teach history at the Manchester Community College, and I help students find jobs. I know—my family knew a lot of people in the area so sometimes I hear of things."

Jessie released a lungful of air. "Oh. For a minute there I thought..." What had she thought? That he was married and had kids. It caused unpleasant feelings to rush through her. But that was foolish. She tried to concentrate on what he'd just said. "You what?"

"Teach."

Jessie leaned back against the booth's tall cushion and laughed that throaty laugh that made Matt smile.

"Why does that make you laugh?"

"Because you don't look like a professor, not that I know a lot of them. But I had you pegged for something else, for a... for an entrepreneur of some sort, or a scientist maybe, or someone who goes around giving sharp advice to important leaders. Or maybe even a trusted family doctor."

"You forgot lawyer and Indian chief."

Jessie laughed again. "Sure. Maybe. But not a teacher."

"Why not?"

She shrugged and looked at him again intently, trying to wrap him up in this new role of teacher. He had a fine, intelligent face. But too carved, too outdoorish somehow, for a teacher. His eyes were too brooding and his hair almost touched the edge of his collar. She still imagined he'd be more comfortable in jeans than in a suit or a corduroy jacket with leather patches on the elbows. But maybe not. She pulled her brows together and continued her scrutiny.

"You're stereotyping, Ms. Sager."

Jessie looked down at the napkin she had folded into a small square. Then she looked back up at him and smiled apologetically. "Sorry. I was. You're right. I think finding out you were a teacher surprised me because I should have known it. I feel as if we've known each other for a lifetime. Do you know what I mean?"

He was beginning to. It was a peculiar thing, this link between them. He felt it and wasn't sure how to deal with it. He wasn't even sure he liked it. At first he had thought it was just Jessie. She had such a magnetism about her that she probably collected people as she walked down the street. But now he wasn't sure. The thought was unsettling. He nodded and drank his coffee.

Jessie went on, intent now on examining the phenomenon. "How do you get to know someone whom you've known forever but just met?"

"I guess you just take it slowly and go back through one incarnation at a time."

"You think I'm silly."

"No, not silly." Matt reached out and without thinking he rested his hand over hers, covering it completely. Her smooth, tan fingers were hidden now in the warm cocoon of his. "Actually you're one of the more interesting young people I've met in a very long time, no matter where we first met, in whichever life or on whichever planet."

"What's with all this *young* business, Matt?"

Matt took a drink of coffee. Then he set the cup back down, leaned his head to one side and looked at her intently. "I guess I feel a need to remind myself." He said the words more to himself than to her.

"Shall I refer to you as Old Matt? Would that help?"

Her teasing slid down inside him more smoothly than fifteen-year-old Scotch. "All right. No more 'Young Jessie.'"

"Thank you." Jessie smiled into his wonderfully brooding eyes. "I'll have to visit the campus someday," she said, moving to a neutral topic.

"You should. It's close by, right through the park."

She nodded.

"It's a nice walk." He looked at his watch. "As a matter of fact, I need to get back there now. If you decide you need some help finding a job, let me know."

She should leave, too. She thought of all the things she had to do: a list of people to contact, some cleanup work still left at the newspaper, and the small matter of a future to plan. She tilted her head sideways and watched as Matt stood up.

He looked down at her. "Well, goodbye—"

"Wait," she said. It was a beautiful day, with a crisp breeze that made her skin tingle. She didn't want to be alone.

"Yes?" Matt said.

"I think I'll come with you."

"Oh" was all Matt answered. The suggestion had surprised him, and the pleasure that followed right after was curious. He frowned, then washed it all away with a stab of reason—he walked casually across the campus with women every day. He smiled politely, paid the check and held open the restaurant door for Jessie.

On the way over Matt insisted they talk about her. What luxury, Jessie thought, even though it made her slightly uncomfortable. Her role was usually that of listener, the helper, the confidante. She had assumed the part so effectively and consistently that acquaintances thought she had every part of her life in control and didn't need help making decisions or examining her motivations.

"About this writing," Matt was saying beside her.

Jessie shoved her hands into the pockets of her billowing yellow skirt. "I've wanted to write forever. Probably when we met in one of those other lives I *was* a writer."

"And most likely a highly successful one," Matt remarked.

"Absolutely," Jess agreed. "Pulitzer, New York Book Award—"

"Movies."

"Sure, if they were already invented."

Their laughter melded together beneath the tangled branches of the fat oak trees.

"All right, back to the here and now," Matt reminded her. He took her arm to guide her around a stump in the middle of the winding pathway. "What kind of writing do you want to do?"

"Well, I've done everything from extolling the virtues of laxatives to an unsuspecting public to writing short stories for the *New Yorker*. I suppose I'd like to do anything within that range."

"The *New Yorker*? I'm very impressed."

"I wrote them *for* the *New Yorker*. I didn't say the *New Yorker* took them."

Matt laughed.

"So let's say I'm versatile."

"Yes," Matt replied, "you are." He slipped his arm over her shoulder. It was a casual gesture, done without thought, but Matt was surprised by the pleasant rush in him as the warmth of her body met his fingers. Aloud he said, "But what's inside of you, Jess? What's clamoring to get out?" There, back to teacher-student talk.

Jessie stumbled over a lumpy root and Matt held her tighter so she wouldn't fall. "Inside me?"

"What does Jessie want to say?"

"Lots of things."

"I thought so."

"But no one is going to pay me for that. At least not today or tomorrow."

"Oh, the money thing'll work out. Don't worry about that. Write what's inside of you."

They were nearing the college and Jessie felt a prickle of irritation. Matt Ridgefield must live in another world. She knew professors weren't usually wealthy, but she suspected he was comfortable. As nice as he was, he didn't understand her dilemma at all. He probably didn't know what medical bills, old debts and back rent were. "How can you say that?" she asked. "'The money thing will work out.' That's foolish, Matt. I'm an optimist, and even I know that's foolish. God helps those who help themselves."

Matt caught the edge of anger in her voice and regretted his words. Sometimes he was too flip about money. It had an evil side and often did cruel things to people. That was one of the reasons Matt had shunned the world of business for teaching. Money simply wasn't a priority for him. He and Jessie were different in that way, he supposed. He didn't spend much, but funds were certainly there if he wanted them. It would mean nothing to him to give her a huge check that would solve all her problems, whatever they were. But already he knew how Jessie Sager would handle such a gesture: the check would be torn to shreds, and he suspected *he* might be as well.

"You're right," he said. "I only meant that it can work out. Maybe I can help you, and then you can stop worrying about money."

"Why?" she asked. "Why are you doing this for me?"

"Damned if I know," Matt mumbled, suddenly gruff. His longtime friend Marilyn Owens said he used that tone of voice whenever he wanted to hide emotion. But what did she know?

He led Jessie up wide stone steps and into the old ivy-covered building that had housed his office for the past twelve years.

"Dena, this is Jessica Sager," Matt said as they walked through his secretary's small office. "Jessie, Dena is my guardian angel. She keeps me out of hell more often than I can say."

Jessie smiled at Dena and noticed the secretary's pleased blush and the adoring look she gave her boss. She also noticed that Matt *didn't* notice. Jessie followed Matt into a wonderfully smelling office, which made her think of leather armchairs, English coffee houses and musty libraries all at once. She looked around carefully and felt a strange intimacy again. The office was Matt Ridgefield. At least a significant part of him. Jessie had decided as they'd walked across the campus that Matt was going to stay in her life for a while, that it was more than a breeze-through, and she needed to learn more about who he was.

Matt busied himself with a stack of messages on his desk, so Jessie was free to indulge her curiosity. Two walls were lined with shelves filled with art pieces and books. Jessie immediately focused on a shelf that held several antique picture frames. The pictures were faded with age. They were mainly of scenery—a forest, a view of the ocean that must have been taken from a boat. She picked up a picture of a towering pine tree with a shining chestnut horse beside it. Next to it were three people, a handsome man next to a beautiful woman with thick loose hair that matched the color of the horse. A young boy of four or five was looking up at the horse, and the adults were looking at the boy. Only the horse seemed aware of the photographer. It was a wonderful picture, a picture of happy people connected in a tender web of love. She placed it back on the shelf and turned around. Matt was watching her with a peculiar expression on his face.

"Most of those are places I've been, places I like."

"I can see why? The pictures are lovely. And the one with the family?"

"I'd forgotten it was there. A friend helped put this office together and she put it there. I was very young."

"It's nice. Your parents are a handsome couple."

"They were, yes. They died a long time ago."

"I'm sorry," Jessie said. "Do you have brothers or sisters?"

"No."

Jessie was listening for more, but Matt had already turned to some papers on his desk, his attention having moved on to other things. That she could understand. She didn't talk easily about her own parents. She glanced back at the picture. The three people made a handsome family, and Jessie suspected that their pasts were very different from her own family's. She moved across the room to where Matt stood.

"I thought it would be like this," she said, her eyes scanning the office.

"What, my desk?"

"No, the room, you. Comfortable, many-faceted."

Matt didn't answer; he just pointed to a chair. "Why don't you sit for a minute. And we'll see about this job business." He sat down.

"Okay," she said, crossing her legs and enjoying the view of Matt across the desk. He pushed back his worn leather chair, his handsome, craggy face never turning away from her.

"I can be just about anything—" she started.

"Like what?"

"Oh, like cook, nanny, writer, clerk, secretary, errand girl, shoe salesman, travel agent—"

"Okay," Matt said. "I get the picture."

"I don't do windows or sell my body or drive semis, but just about anything in between is a go."

Matt was still. The sunlight behind him had crept past the tangled vines outside his window and cast a lovely glow on Jessie's vibrant face. It took his breath away. And in the next instant, before he'd even had time to record the full beauty of her features, a sudden, almost painful, rush of desire coursed through him.

"Professor?" It was Dena with a timely entrance. Matt pushed himself forward in the chair. He swallowed hard, then looked up, his brows pulling together in stern concentration. "Yes, Dena?"

"Sorry to interrupt you, but your History of Ideas class is in ten minutes."

Matt looked at his watch. "You're right." He nodded calmly at his secretary and shuffled an already neat stack of papers. Then he stood and looked at Jessie, who had already risen and was shaking her head.

"History of Ideas," she said. "I'm impressed. That sounds like heady stuff."

Matt smiled. He was in control again, but the effect of Jessie was still there, just beneath his skin. Young Jessie, he silently told himself. *As young as some of my students.* He reached for his glasses and pipe with one hand.

Jessie noticed that both items fit in his palm. He had such nice hands, she thought. Large and tan and rough. Yes, his hands were rough. That's unusual for a professor, she decided.

"We didn't finish, though," Matt said as he picked up a briefcase and strode toward the door. "Would you want to, ah, how about if I pick you up for dinner and we figure this out?" While the words were coming out of his mouth, Matt was wondering at them. *He didn't even know this woman; what was he doing?*

"I can't, Matt," Jessie answered. And then she added with a hint of teasing in her voice, "A friend promised me a celebration dinner for my entry into show biz."

"Well, the effort sure deserves a celebration," Matt said, his face relaxing into a smile. "Be sure you give your friend a complete replay."

"Oh, I'll certainly do that!"

"Is this friend someone special in your life?"

"Very. A good friend."

"Is he...ah..." Matt stood still at the door, not quite looking Jessie in the eye. His brow was furrowed and he concentrated on the large woven purse that hung heavily from her narrow shoulder.

Jessie laughed and walked through the door ahead of Matt. "No, he's not. A close friend, that's all. A friend, not a lover."

"Can't someone be both?"

"Sure. And when I find one of those, I'm going to marry him," Jessie announced, "*if* he can afford me and wants a houseful of kids. But this friend happens to be married already."

Matt listened with half an ear, his attention caught on the mention of family. That's what he would have expected: Jessie with a houseful of kids, and easy, relaxed love oozing out all over the place. They'd be happy kids. She'd be a great mother. He tried to put a man in the scenario next to Jessie, but he couldn't put a face on the figure.

They were nearing the wide entrance doors to the building now and Matt glanced down at his watch. He was never late for class, a standard he had unconsciously set for himself sometime in his career. Today was a first, and there was no conscience stepping in to give him hell. He shrugged his shoulders and held the door open for Jessie. When she brushed lightly against his chest, he smiled and breathed in the fresh smell of her hair. No, one more day with Jessie wouldn't matter much in the grand scheme of things.

"So when should we do it then?" he said to Jessie.

For a minute Jessie had to think about what he meant. Her mind was busy with other things, including a brief analysis of the feel of Matt's body as she'd stepped through the door. She brushed up against people like that all the time, on elevators, streets, and in crowded department stores. There was nothing intimate about it at all. But brushing up against Matt Ridgefield *was* intimate. Sexual. And that was strange.

"Tomorrow night?" Matt was asking beside her.

"Tomorrow night?" Jessie turned and looked at him. "Oh, the job thing. I promised my soon-to-be ex-boss I'd clean out the office this week. They want to rent it, I guess. They're going to pay me extra for it."

Matt nodded.

"You don't really have to do this. You're not responsible or anything."

Matt shrugged. "I don't know. I guess I figure you'll spend all day in that bagel store drowning your sorrows in pickles and bread dough if I don't help you find a job."

"There are worse fates. Acting, for instance." Jessie gave a short throaty laugh.

"Seriously," Matt said, "I'd like to help."

She straightened her head and met his eyes. "You do, don't you? I don't know why, but I appreciate it. Tell you what, give me the week to get my head on straight. How about the end of the week?"

"Saturday?" he asked.

"Perfect." She fished out an old sales receipt from her purse and scribbled down a phone number. "Call me, tell me where and when, and I'll be there."

"Provided there's food."

"Goes without saying," Jessie replied, and the wonderful throaty laugh that followed stayed in Matt's mind across the small campus and into the classroom where twenty students were diligently watching the clock, waiting the requisite twenty minutes for a late teacher until they could pour out of the room and enjoy a free hour in the sunshine.

Three

But Saturday came and went without Jessie Sager. She had left a message with Dena on Friday that Saturday wouldn't work after all. She was terribly sorry, the message had said, but she'd call sometime the next week.

Matt was disappointed and found his disappointment irritating. Who was Jessie Sager anyway? She was a nice young woman, an interesting person. An acquaintance who made him laugh and feel years younger. Which was what she was. Nearly *fifteen years* younger, as a matter of fact.

Matt vowed to set his mind in order and he moved through the weekend fulfilling commitments: a lecture Friday night and a cocktail party with Marilyn on Saturday night at the Twin Oaks Country Club. He had known Marilyn since childhood and they could count on each other whenever an escort or companion was needed.

Going to Twin Oaks and sitting in its mauve-and-gray elegance was never Matt's first choice of things to do. It was the world he was raised in and had left behind with relief. But it was Marilyn's world, too, so he went, and he sat beneath the stars on the gaslit patio while uniformed waiters catered to him, and he thought about Jessie Sager.

"Hi."

Jessie's husky voice on the phone drew Matt out of his thoughts.

He was sitting at his office desk staring out the window at the fascinating change of seasons. Autumn was settling in with its amazing colors and textures. It was hard to remember that weeks before he had been walking through fields in the country with the hot sun beating down on his bare back. "Hi, Jessie," he said.

"You sound thoughtful."

"It's the weather. The changes—"

"I know," she agreed softly. "That's what life's about."

She sounded sad, Matt thought. There was a lilt missing in her voice. "Are you all right, Jessie?"

"I'm fine. But I would like to see you. I thought I could handle this job by myself, but I've struck out. Would you help me?"

"I'll try, Jessie," he replied. He felt that strange tug in his gut again. "I know of a few possibilities. Just say the word—"

"You're a friend, Matt." She spoke so quietly that Matt felt, rather than heard, her words.

Later that afternoon, Matt walked to the campus cafeteria. Jessie had suggested meeting there because it would be the least inconvenient spot for him. He got to the crowded place first and settled himself at a table near the wall of windows so he could see Jessie coming. But when she finally walked up the sidewalk, his head was lowered in a book and he missed her entrance.

Jessie spotted Matt immediately. She stood outside for a minute, looking at him through the wide windows. She'd had quite a week. Between the job mess and her volunteer work at the orphanage where she'd met little Emma, she was feeling drained. But seeing Matt there, his head down, his face thoughtful, brought a pleasant hum back to her body and spirit. She felt a sense of well-being. Seeing him made her think that everything in the world would work out all right. Matt moved his head slightly and the sunlight caught a tiny fleck of gray in his hair, making it glisten like wet silk. Jessie smiled for the first time that day and went inside.

"I'm sorry I'm late," she said, coming up beside Matt.

Matt's head lifted. "That's okay. It's good to see you."

Jessie sat down quickly, leaving her jacket on. "It's getting colder."

He nodded. He was too busy looking at the drawn expression on her lovely face to concentrate on comments about the weather. "Jessie, you look awful."

"Thanks." She half smiled. "What is it with you, Matt? First you convince me I should be a model, then you tell me I need help in the beauty department. Okay, which is it?"

The words put energy back into her face. Matt smiled. "You definitely don't need any help in the beauty department. Now let me order you something and then we can get down to business. You sounded a little desperate on the phone."

Jessie began to relax. Again, that nice feeling of security washed over her. She didn't want to question it too severely for fear it wouldn't hold up beneath the scrutiny.

"I'm not desperate," she said. "But a little more anxious than I was the other day. Old cocky Jess thought she'd walk right into the presidency of First National." She laughed.

"It's their loss," Matt said.

"I think that's what they were afraid of," Jessie joked.

Matt laughed, and then wondered at the ease with which he did that in her presence. He pulled a sheet of paper from his pocket. "Here are some possibilities. Let's have a go at it."

Jessie watched while Matt carefully went over the list of positions. He smoothed the paper with one tan hand, and with the other he went through each item point by point.

"Now," Matt said after the brief explanation of the last job, "which ones interest you most?"

"The one that pays the best," Jessie answered.

"Do you mean that?"

"Yes. I told you I need money, Matt. I hate to bring it up so bluntly and so often, but that's the truth."

"Okay."

"And besides, this isn't a career we're looking at here. It's only a way for me to keep the ends from fraying right now. The more money, the less fray."

"So you want a temporary job?"

"I don't know," she said. She shook her head and looked slightly irritated, as if she didn't want to be bothered with details. "I might stay with it for years if my needs stay the same and it fills them. But I don't want to think about the future right now, Matt, I just want a job. I'll think about the future tomorrow."

"All right." Matt backed off a little. Something was eating at Jessie, but he knew she wasn't going to talk about it now, so he concentrated on the job list. "There's sev-

eral here that will pay well but might not take you anywhere."

Jessie smiled. "That's okay. I'm not ready to go anywhere."

Good, Matt thought. "Then I'll circle them and you can
check them out."

"It's a deal."

They shook hands then, spontaneously, their palms
pressing together over the tortoiseshell tabletop. And their
tentative, slightly uncomfortable laughter came at the same
time. They got up to get some food, and just as they were
sitting back down with their double burgers and shakes,
Marilyn walked in.

"Matthew!" she said, gliding over to their table. "Dena
thought I might find you here." The elegant woman
looked down at Jessie and smiled. "Hello."

"Hello." Jessie managed to smile back. For a moment
she felt totally intimidated by the gorgeous blonde with the
imposing stance. She glanced at Matt.

"Jessie," he said, "meet Marilyn Owens. An old friend
of mine."

"*Old* friend, my eye," Marilyn argued, frowning.

Even when she frowned, Jessie thought, she was beautiful. She was about Matt's age and stood tall with the
gracious air of one who knew the world would never cross
her. Her suit was gorgeous, her shoes the kind whose price
made Jessie dizzy, and there was an air of complete elegance about her.

"All right," Matt conceded, accommodating Marilyn
with an easy smile. "Jessie, this is Marilyn, a not-so-old
friend."

"And Jessie," Marilyn said, "you must be one of
Matt's students."

Jessie's husky laugh floated over their half-eaten burgers. "Oh, no," she countered. "I'm not a student."

Matt looked uncomfortable. "No, Marilyn," he added, "Jessie and I are simply friends. Do you want to join us?"

Marilyn paused for a moment, as if trying to figure something out. Finally she shook her head with a small gesture that made her smooth golden hair bounce in slow motion. It reminded Jessie of an ad for shampoo. "Thanks, Matt, but I can't," Marilyn replied. "I only stopped by to tell you I won't be able to make that theater date tonight. I feel terrible about the short notice."

"No problem."

"Good. I knew you'd understand." She lifted one brow and looked from Matt to the food on the table and back to Matt's face. "You'll put on weight with those shakes."

Matt shrugged. "I haven't had a milk shake in a long time. It tastes great."

Jessie laughed but felt strangely guilty for being a bad influence on Matt. Was drinking shakes a bad thing to do when you were over thirty?

There was an awkward pause then, but Jessie was sure that Marilyn didn't feel it. She registered no unease at all. Jessie couldn't imagine her ever being uncomfortable. Then she wondered where Marilyn fitted into Matt's life, and realized with a start that her wonderings carried emotions with them.

Marilyn smiled, breaking up Jessie's thoughts. "Jessie," she said, "it was nice meeting you."

"Thank you. And you, too, Ms. Owens." Jessie realized she sounded like an adolescent!

"Oh, call me Marilyn, please." The tall, together-looking woman turned to Matt. "And now I'm off for an emergency meeting at the publisher's. We're still trying to work out the snags."

"The book?" Matt inquired.

"Don't worry." Marilyn patted him on the shoulder. "It will work out."

Matt seemed lost in thought. "I'm not worried," he said. "It's your project, not mine."

"Good. And now I have to go. You and Jessie can sit here and bask in cholesterol, but I have things to do." She kissed Matt lightly on the cheek, waved at Jessie and was off, a flash of slender loveliness in the cluttered college cafeteria.

Jessie watched her walk away. "She's lovely."

"Who?" Matt asked.

Jessie looked at him curiously. "Marilyn, of course."

"Oh, sure," he said distractedly. He was scribbling something on the top of the list of job possibilities. "I just had another idea, Jessie. You might want to try this number first. I know the pay is good, and I think you'd be good at the job."

Jessie waited until Saturday to call Matt.

Bourke and Bailey, the company with whom she had interviewed at Matt's suggestion, was a small publishing house, and the job, which Matt obviously knew about all along, was assisting in the research for and writing of a biography of an early mayor of Manchester, a man named Alexander Richard Ridgefield. And Jessie would be working with a woman whose name happened to be Marilyn Owens. One grand bushel basket full of coincidences. Except Jessie didn't believe in coincidences and she was as sure as she breathed that Matt had talked Bourke and Bailey into hiring her. They could have gotten someone with far more experience, at least on paper. Jessie wasn't sure how she felt about it at first, but then decided she'd do an excellent job, so why should she worry about how she got it? Bourke and Bailey would certainly get their money's worth.

Her fingers were itching to write something substantial. The pay was excellent, and the hours were flexible. She could continue her work at the orphanage and be there for Emma, now that the little girl needed her more than ever. Maybe everything would turn out all right in the world, and maybe Matt Ridgefield was one rabbit's foot that would keep her life on even keel for a while.

So Jessie did what instinct dictated: she snatched up the job before any of the principals had a chance to change his or her mind.

It was perhaps ungrateful not to call and let Matt know she had gotten the position, but Jessie decided she needed to straighten out her emotions on all this first. He was a friend, one of those rare ones you recognized from the start, regardless of age or background. He was older, undoubtedly wiser and a good person to add balance to her life.

Yes, she decided late Friday night as she sat in the window of her small apartment and watched the moon fill in the black sky. That's what Matt was: a kind, wise, older friend; the big brother she'd never had.

No sooner had she concluded this than images of Marilyn and Matt flitted across her mind. Were they lovers? There was an ease between them that was unmistakable, the ease of two people who know each other very well. How well? And why were the thoughts uncomfortable and why did they remind her of the delicious sensations that has passed through her body when her kind, wise, big-brother-like friend touched her?

Sleep was restless and punctuated by a dream that Jessie resolved to tell no one about. The books said you were allowed such fantasies, and it didn't matter if the costar was someone as unlikely and impossible as Matt Ridge-field because it was only a dream, after all.

"But a dream that packed an incredible wallop," Jessie muttered early the next morning as she stood, alone and still tired, in her small, cluttered apartment. Dust motes leapt through the air. She plugged in the coffeepot and began bending toward the floor to stretch out her still-sleepy body. Before the exercises were completed she had planned the day: clean, drink coffee, move into her new office and thank Matt for being kind. The order of those things was up for grabs.

Matt stopped in his tracks when the phone rang in Dena's office. Dena didn't come in on Saturdays and the ringing was a harsh invasion of the still office.

"Matt," said the voice, "this is Jessie."

"Hi. I had given you up for lost. How was your week?" He lifted one shoulder, stretching out the unused muscles.

"I got a job, Matt, thanks to you. Which is why I'm calling, to thank you."

"No need, but congratulations. I'm glad, Jessie." He'd known she'd got the job because he'd told Frederick Bourke, an old family friend, that he'd be crazy not to give Jessie a chance. But to hear her voice was what he really wanted. Seeing her wouldn't be bad either. "Would you like to celebrate with a bagel and cup of coffee?"

"No, Matt. I've taken enough of your time. I don't want to impose on your weekend as well."

"No imposition. I just finished a meeting here at school and was about to leave and head for the country. Some coffee would keep me awake on the road."

"Well, I'll tell you what. Marilyn is going to show me my office in a while and I'm going to move some things in. It's over near your college—"

"I know."

"So I could meet you there if you'd like, and the coffee will be my treat. I'll share my thermos with you."

"Sounds serious."

"Yes. Real java beans, which I only share with special people."

"How could I refuse?"

Jessie met Matt and Marilyn in less than thirty minutes. They were waiting at the door; Marilyn had the keys. The publishing offices were in an old stone house adjacent to the campus and Jessie loved it on sight. The doors squeaked and, inside, the desks were old and smelled of linseed oil. The office Marilyn pointed Jessie toward used to be someone's dining room, complete with a large bay window and a plump cushioned seat beneath it. They set Jessie's boxes on the floor near the desk.

"How will I work here?" Jessie asked. She looked around the room and felt she'd been there all her life. "It's so comfortable."

"You'll work just fine," Marilyn said. She opened a cupboard and ran a finger along the surface, then closed it, satisfied. "I'm a tough task master."

Matt, standing beside Marilyn, nodded in mock agreement. He was wearing a pair of slacks today, far more casual than the other times Jessie had seen him, but there was still a formality about him that she wanted to peel away. Jeans, she thought, pushing her hands down into the pockets of her own faded pair. Old jeans and a plaid shirt, that would do it. Aloud she said, "Well, shall we toast this whole thing with a cup of Jessie's finest?"

Marilyn laughed and excused herself. She was off, she explained, to her late husband's family farm for a weekend "gathering."

"That means uniformed butlers and tables groaning under the weight of food, planned activities following the early afternoon rest period, which follows the champagne lunch, and a small orchestra for the evening," Matt explained to Jessie as they waved goodbye to Marilyn from the front porch of the house-turned-office.

"Her late husband?" Jessie asked, pulling apart the offered pieces of information. She'd check up on the champagne lunch in good time.

"Marilyn was married for a few years to Ford Owens. He was a great guy. We all went to school together. He died in a auto accident eight years ago."

"How awful for her. And she hasn't remarried?"

"Nope," Matt said as they walked back inside.

Jessie waited for Matt to say more, but instead he busied himself pouring coffee. Carefully he carried the plastic cups over to the window seat and changed the subject. "How does the job sound to you?"

"It sounds fantastic," Jessie said, kicking off her shoes and curling her feet beneath her on the window seat. "But now, sir, you have a few questions to answer."

Matt sat facing her, his back resting on the side wall. He sipped his coffee slowly, waiting for her to go on. It bothered Jessie a little, the way he did that, never offering information, only giving her what she asked for.

"So tell me, Matt," she went on, "why aren't *you* writing the definitive biography of this man who happens to be your grandfather."

"Great-grandfather."

"No matter. Why aren't you?"

"Because I'm not a writer, and I have no desire to write a biography of anyone, especially one of my relatives."

Jessie looked up sharply. She had been concentrating on the built-in bookcase, mentally placing her pictures and books and plants on it. The tone in Matt's voice brought her full attention back to the conversation. "Oh?"

Matt's voice smoothed out. "I only meant the book isn't my project, nor was it my idea. I help when I'm asked, provide family documents, that sort of thing. But that's all."

"Well, I'm looking forward to meeting the Honorable Alexander Richard Ridgefield," Jessie said.

"You'll probably like him. He was a free-spirited person, kind of like you. And I have no doubt you'll do a good job with his life. Marilyn is doing a good job managing the project, I hear, but she's not a writer and the guy they had counted on moved to Wisconsin."

Jessie watched Matt as he talked. His eyes were so deep, so beautiful. They were the color of space, clear and fathomless. As hard as she tried, she couldn't see into the depths beyond the beauty. "I see," she said slowly.

"This coffee is just what I needed. And to see that you're settled." He got up rather abruptly and looked down at Jessie. Sitting curled like that, her body drenched in sunlight, she looked younger than she was. Matt swallowed hard around the feeling that had collected into a lump in his throat. "I need to go now," he said.

"Oh, sure," Jessie said. She walked beside him to the door. "I'm glad you came. It's right that you should be here today since this is all because of you, Matt. You dropped into my life, and all of a sudden I have a job, an office—" she hooked her arm through his as they stepped onto the front porch "—and not to mention a good friend."

Matt was staring over her shoulder and beyond the bushes toward his Jeep, which was parked at the curb. He was trying hard to concentrate on the rest of the day, on the time he'd spend out in the country, feeling the wind on his face and the sun beating down on his back. Being alone. It was the time he coveted most. But his thoughts were clouded, unfocused.

Jessie looked up at him. She could feel something happening: the physical sensation of touching Matt. The contact took on a life of its own, spinning off swirls of feeling that invaded her body.

Matt looked down at her and started to speak, but the closeness of her face was too much.

He lifted her chin with two fingers, tipping it up that last inch so that when he covered her lips with his own, it was a perfect kiss, passionate and total.

Jessie felt her knees begin to buckle. The emotions were swirling faster and faster, sending her whole body spinning. She grabbed his arms for support, but the kiss continued. Her lips opened slightly and Matt responded, his tongue dipping inside until Jessie couldn't breathe. She thought she was going to explode.

At last Matt released her. He stepped away abruptly and took a deep breath. His unsmiling eyes held her there against the railing of the porch. "Well," he said, "you have a lot to do and I have to go. Congratulations on the job, Jessie."

Later, alone in the sunny office, Jessie realized she hadn't answered him. She had simply stood there, leaning against the porch pillar for support, watching him walk away. He got into his car and didn't look back. She saw his hand fork roughly through his hair, saw him lean his head back for a minute as if to regain strength, and then he gunned the engine fiercely. She saw tiny pebbles scatter beneath the spin of the wheels, and he was gone. She didn't even know to where. The country, he had said. There was a lot of that.

She sat on the window seat and stared through the window, then at her desk, the boxes, the empty bookshelves. But she only saw Matt's face the way it appeared the instant before he kissed her, his eyes smoky with desire. And then the harsh, almost angry way he looked when he walked away.

Matt Ridgefield was not a simple man.

Four

—

"Marilyn, how long have you known Matt?" It was Saturday afternoon and Jessie sat at her desk typing a profile of Alexander Ridgefield. Sunlight splashed across the hardwood floor of her office and Marilyn walked through it to peer over Jessie's shoulder.

"How can you do that, Jessie—talk and write? You must have two brains." Marilyn watched the green words appear on the computer monitor. "I've known Matt for as long as I can remember. His nanny and mine were friends and we used to buggy over to the park together."

Jessie laughed. "Buggy buddies—sounds like fun."

"Yes, it was, I guess." Marilyn continued to read the screen. In the two weeks the women had been working together, they had unexpectedly developed a friendship. Marilyn had obviously considered Jessie far too young to be considered a friend, and Jessie had been so unnerved by the older woman's poise and beauty that she had assumed she should speak only in respectful tones and be seen and not heard. But almost instantly the disparities had dissolved in mutual respect and enjoyment in one another's company.

"And you went to school together?"

"Brother and sister academies. Coed wasn't the way to go in private schools back then." Marilyn pointed to a paragraph on the screen. "This is good, Jessie. You've really captured the spirit of Alexander Ridgefield."

Jessie followed her pointing finger. "Thank you. And you have masterfully changed the subject."

"Sorry. It wasn't intentional, but I do think that Matt is the kind of person you need to discover firsthand. What I know of Matt isn't relevant, except to me, and the same goes for you."

Jessie accepted the wise hedge. Marilyn was right; she shouldn't be asking questions about Matt. She didn't usually give in to that level of curiosity, but somehow the words materialized without thought. Matt had totally disappeared from her life since the day he'd kissed her and driven off into the country or wherever he was going. But he preyed on her mind, leaving her limp and tired after a full night's sleep. Working on the book about his greatgrandfather didn't help a whit because Matt bore a striking resemblance to the dashing first mayor of Manchester, whose pictures now cluttered her office.

The worst part of the whole thing was, she missed him. She didn't know if it was simply his presence, or the sexual tension that turned her mind to mush, or his incredible, searching eyes, but she did know she missed him.

"I will say this, Jess," Marilyn was saying, almost as an afterthought, "Matt Ridgefield has drawn tight lines around his life over the years. And he doesn't step over them easily, if ever." She looked through some papers, put them back on Jessie's desk and looked at her with a new smile. "That was said as a friend. Speaking as project director, I think you work too much. So scoot. You shouldn't use up your whole Saturday like this, and there's very little left."

Jessie tucked Marilyn's first comment into a corner of her mind. She would think about it later. She shook her head in response to the second message. "No, it's only fair. You've been great about letting me continue volunteering at the orphanage and I want to make sure I give Bourke and Bailey its due."

"You do, my friend, you do."

The ring of the telephone interrupted the conversation. Marilyn reached over and answered it while Jessie slipped down the hall to find more paper for her printer.

When she returned, Marilyn was standing, putting her things together. "Jessie, today we practice the Golden Rule."

Jessie busied herself with fitting paper into the printer. "Which one is that? The way I see it, most everyone has his or her own Golden Rule. And they change. Today mine is Love thy Computer. I'm becoming totally attached to this little guy."

Marilyn laughed and walked toward the the door. "Well, mine is Love thy neighbor, etcetera. I'm leaving, therefore you are, too. Scat."

Jessie straightened. "Marilyn, I've concluded over these weeks that your brains matched your beauty. Now I'm not so sure."

"Seriously, I'm closing shop for the day. No arguments accepted. Out."

She was holding Jessie's purse in one hand and had the other over the light switch. Jessie looked at her curiously, then laughed. "What is this, some secret rendezvous you've planned and you need to get rid of witnesses?"

"Jessie, shame. You're far too young for such lascivious thoughts." She dropped the purse on the table. "The fact is, you looked strained and we can't have strained writers at Bourke and Bailey. It's unacceptable. And hearing about your work at St. Bede's Orphanage has made me think you need time to relax."

"Marilyn, that's silly. I thrive on tension. Honest. If I'm not busy, I go crazy."

"So be busy relaxing for a few hours. That's what I told Matt—"

"Matt?"

"Matt. When he returned my call just now."

"Oh." Why did hearing his name cause the green words to jump on the screen?

Marilyn went on, "He's coming by to see that you get out of here and enjoy the sunshine."

"That's not necessary," Jessie said. For some reason she was irritated. "I'll leave if you like but Matt doesn't have to play baby-sitter."

"Jessie, I'm sorry if it sounded that way—"

Jessie turned off the computer. "I just don't want to tie Matt up, that's all. He's obviously busy."

"No one manipulates Matt. I wouldn't worry about making demands on his time."

Jessie started to argue further but stopped before the words came out. She was making too much of this. She'd simply handle it when Matt came by. She bit down on her bottom lip and willed away the butterflies playing havoc with her insides.

Marilyn left a few minutes later, her peach-colored Herrara jacket tossed elegantly over one shoulder. "I'll see you Monday," she said as she breezed through the door. "Tell Matt hello."

"Sure," Jessie replied, pulling her papers into a neat stack. She straightened a few books on the bookshelf, and then concentrated on the photo of Alexander Ridgefield at his first mayoral inauguration. "Okay, Alexander," she said. She touched the yellowed photo with the tip of her finger. "You have some explaining to do because those are some of your genes in Matt's gorgeous body."

"Hello, Jessie," Matt said from the doorway.

Jessie spun around and the picture floated to the floor. "Don't do that! You scared the heck out of me."

Matt strode across the room and picked up the picture. "Sorry. But the door was open."

Jessie couldn't speak. She watched him as he bent over, then straightened back up just a few feet in front of her. Her breath left her body.

"Is that really you?" Her voice was strained.

"Who were you expecting?"

"I was expecting the professor." She looked at his face and gave him a slight smile before continuing her inspection. The top two buttons of his plaid shirt were undone and revealed a dark thatch of hair that curled slightly over the fabric. The sleeves were rolled up to his elbows and his arms showed the result of physical work or exercise. In faded, worn jeans, Matt looked incredibly sexy, and far more like a Wyoming cowboy than a Connecticut professor. This is the way her mind imagined him days ago. Today Matt looked completely comfortable. And the effect on Jessie was considerable and disturbing. "Well," she said with a peculiar catch in her voice. "You look nice."

Matt looked at her curiously. "Thank you. So do you."

"I mean it. It's a whole other you. But I saw it, I think, that first day. Beneath the suit and tie and glasses, I saw something else."

"Maybe this is how we met in one of those other lives," he said. "You talking to old pictures and me in my old jeans."

"No," she said as her heartbeat raced. "This I would have remembered."

"So how are you?" Matt leaned back against the desk, the picture of his great-grandfather still in his hand.

She nodded, her eyes examining the wavy shadow across his shoulder. "Fine. Job's great."

"Good. Been busy?"

She nodded again.

"Marilyn says you work too hard."

"That's just Marilyn. She wants me to have bankers' hours."

"Oh. Well, maybe you should."

An awkward silence settled between them then and it irritated Jessie. It was an intrusion into the easiness she had enjoyed with Matt before. "Damn," she said aloud.

"Pardon?" Matt crossed his arms and looked at her. His thick brows lifted.

"It was the kiss. The feelings. That's what sexual tension does." Her cheeks pinked as she talked, but her expression was one hundred percent serious. "It changes things."

She looked so upset that Matt instinctively reached out to touch her. A thought made him pull his hand back. He hadn't known how he'd feel seeing her again. He had stayed away intentionally, busying himself in his classes, a lecture to the Kiwanis club. That was the stuff his life was made of. Some would say his middle-aged life. It wasn't made up of a woman years younger, a carefree, spirited woman who was just beginning to reach for her goals, and who didn't fit into his chosen life-style by any stretch of the imagination.

"I'm sorry," Matt finally said. "I took advantage of the situation the other day. It seemed right at the time."

"Maybe that's part of the problem."

Matt knew what she meant. It felt right, but it wasn't. Jessie was young and vulnerable and not the kind of person to come out of a casual affair painlessly.

"Let's get out of here, Jess," Matt said abruptly. "Fresh air is what you need."

She followed him wordlessly, pulling the door closed behind her until she heard it lock. Was that what she needed, to be healed? Maybe so. Maybe the curls of fire that burned in her were an illness. Fresh air would tamp the embers down until there was nothing there but smooth, uncomplicated friendship. She followed him to the Jeep and slid onto the high seat beside him. "Kiss or no kiss, I've missed seeing you, Matt."

"Well, I thought it might be best to put some distance between us and see if I could reappear in your life as a wise old friend." He started up the car and headed down the tree-shaded street.

"We gave up that 'old' stuff a while ago."

"I forgot."

"Well, we'll just have to see how this goes, Professor, see what happens."

"I guess."

"Where have you been in your John Wayne duds?"

"The country. I came in just for a few hours."

Later Matt supposed that that was what planted the idea in his mind, that small mention of where he'd been, and where he'd still be if he hadn't had a meeting with the dean that couldn't be arranged for any other day but Saturday.

But for whatever reason, when Jessie suggested a drive, he found himself maneuvering the Jeep out of city traffic and onto the quiet, dusty roads of the surrounding countryside.

Jessie leaned back and breathed in the piny smell that clung to the seats of the Jeep. "Oh, Matt, this is wonderful. I can feel every inch of me loosening up. It's grand."

"The country does that. I'm not a believer in a lot of spiritual kinds of things, but there's a real magic out here."

"Yes, there is. Your great-grandfather was most at home in the country, too."

"So I hear. Especially a part of the country that used to hold a famous little tavern in Green County. He nearly supported it single-handedly people say."

"Well, yes, that too," Jessie said, remembering the accounts she'd read of Alexander Ridgefield's penchant for good times and women. "But he also loved to ride his horse along the river. It's where he planned all his projects, out there all alone, without any interference. I think it's interesting that he was the mayor of a city, responsible for its growth and success, and it seems he was truly himself only when he got away from all that."

"I didn't know that about him. Maybe those are the genes that found their way to me."

Jessie blushed. So he'd heard her comments earlier. "Maybe," she said quickly. "There are others, too."

"Oh?"

"You're built like him. He had lighter hair, but you have the same brooding look in your eye, the same fire lurking beneath the skin."

Matt stirred, uncomfortable. "You can tell all that from some black-and-white pictures?"

"And his diary." Jessie was warming to her subject and she talked with quick animation. "The main difference in the two of you—as I see it, anyway—is that the mayor had a devil-may-care streak in him. An openness to experience, good and bad.''

Matt had lifted his hand from the wheel and settled it on her knee. ''Those are strong statements you're backhandedly making about me, Jessie Sager.''

She looked over at him. He was half smiling. ''Well, as I said, it's only my humble opinion.''

''Okay. You're entitled to that.''

He made no attempt to challenge her, but Jessie knew that didn't mean anything. He was probably enjoying her misconceptions, if that's what they were. But he *was* reserved and cautious and a bunch of other things that seemed to Jessie to be too carefully acted out to be real. That's what Marilyn was talking about, she supposed, those secrets each person found out for him or herself. Maybe she'd find out and maybe she wouldn't. She directed her gaze through the windshield. ''Where are we, Matt? These are roads I've never taken.''

''Not many people take them. That's why I like them.''

''From the sinking sun over there, I'd say we're heading northeast.''

''The lady is a trailblazer.''

''Camp Fire Girl. For one year.''

''Why only one?'' Matt took a right turn and drove carefully down a two-lane road lined with spruce and pine.

''One was enough,'' Jessie answered. That was all it had taken for Josh Sager to make the young Jessie realize that she didn't belong in groups, and that no matter how much she told herself she was like everyone else, she wasn't. Who else brought a father to the father-daughter Camp Fire banquet who filled his coffee cup over and over again with Scotch?

''You didn't like it?''

"Parents had to be involved. And my father drank too much. He told a string of X-rated jokes that were a little hard to live down. At age nine anyway. And then he passed out on top of me."

"That's tough," Matt said. He felt a familiar anger rise up in him that was bigger than the conversation allowed, and he quickly swallowed the sour taste that coated his throat. "Hey, look over there." He slowed the Jeep down to a crawl.

Jessie followed the direction of his finger. A few yards from the road, a single deer glided noiselessly across a small green clearing. Its feet didn't seem to touch the ground. It stopped, head back and ears alert. Then it was off again. The graceful flight appeared in the small opening in the woods for only a few lovely seconds, and then the deer was gone, swallowed up by the dark shadows of the pine trees.

Jessie didn't speak. The moment swelled with communication and she felt filled by it. It even seemed significant that it followed the brief reference to her father, like a sorbet to wash away an unwanted taste.

Matt drove on, rounding the curve in the road, which he was as familiar with as his own body. He was close to the farm now and knew that was probably where he'd been headed all along. It was a strange turn of events, because he'd never shared this part of his life. Applewood was his protection, his haven. Even Marilyn had never seen his place. He looked over at Jessie. Her head was back against the seat, her eyes focused on the passing scenery in a trusting, dreamy way. The silence between them was comfortable and easy now, like a soft blanket.

"Where does this road lead to?" Jessie asked a short while later. She was fascinated by the flashes of color along the roadside. The bright oranges, reds and golds of the autumn palette. There were some houses here, set far back, many with picket fences lining the road and marking the hilly properties.

The innocent question triggered an uncomfortable sensation in Matt, but he buried it as quickly as it appeared. He wasn't going to think about where this was leading. One day in the country with Jessie certainly couldn't bring any drastic twists to his life, or to hers.

"Picnic grounds?" Jessie asked, her curiosity piqued now.

"Nope," Matt said.

Jessie sat up straighter and spotted the mailbox standing tall and straight beside a white gate. M. Ridgefield, it said. Another sign, cut in the shape of a tree and attached to the fence, said Applewood.

Jessie looked beyond it, over the fence and up the long winding gravel drive. Tall pines lined the road and she looked through the webbed fan of their branches to a rambling white house set back against the brilliant blue sky. A group of apple trees was off to the right.

"Cerulean" was all she said.

"What?" Matt looked over at her. Her eyes were wide as she took in the house, yard and woods in the background.

"The color of the sky," she explained.

"Oh." He guessed this meant she liked the place, but he couldn't be sure. He stopped briefly to take some letters out of the mailbox, then drove on, his elbow still resting on the door, his eyes straight ahead, his face peaceful. No violent force shook him and threw him out of the Jeep, so he knew it was all right. Maybe people *should* come to this house. Jessie seemed to fit okay.

Jessie didn't say a word while Matt parked the car in front of the two-story house. Then she finally released the sigh that had been building up inside her chest.

Matt looked at her sharply. "Are you all right?"

But Jessie had already tumbled out of the Jeep and was scanning the house and its shutters. Her glance darted over to the pond that was barely visible around the side of the house, and then came back to rest on the front of the house. There was a huge lump in her throat.

It was *her* house, the one in her childhood dreams, the one that had protected her and soothed her. It had taken on such a clear reality over the years that sometimes she'd find a piece of furniture at an antique sale and have to dig her fingers into her palms to keep from buying it for the front bedroom or the living room or the airy back porch. She knew all the details—which room had eyelet curtains, where the old four-poster bed would be placed against the creamy bedroom wall, how many ducks made their home in the pond, where the apple trees were that the children would climb. Her heart beat crazily.

"Do you like it?" Matt asked, standing beside her. She looked strange, he thought. Maybe it *had* been a mistake to bring someone here.

Jessie walked toward the house, still not speaking.

"Hey, Jess," he said, a hand on her shoulder to stop her. "What gives here?"

Jessie looked up at him, her eyes glistening.

"What's wrong?"

She shook her head. "Wrong? Oh, I'm sorry, Matt. I'm acting like a dolt!"

"No, not a dolt. A little strange maybe."

"It's this house, Matt." She looked back at it and then calmed herself. She sounded absurd. How could she explain this to Matt? It was crazy. "As a kid," she began slowly, "I imagined my dream house—I guess a lot of little girls do that—and this is it. That's all. It became so real to me over the years that I knew it existed somewhere. But it was still a surprise to find it."

She faced Matt.

He was listening to her closely, not in a patronizing way, and his lips curved in a pleased, half smile. "I think that means you like my house," he said. He draped his arm across her shoulders. He'd made the right choice in having Jessie Sager be his first houseguest.

Jessie nodded. "It also means I want to see every inch of it. In my dreams I couldn't see behind the trees, or over toward the pond."

They walked for more than two hours, first around the house and pond where Jessie was surprised to find far more ducks than she'd imagined, and then across the meadow and along the border of spruce and pine trees that made a natural windbreak for the big house. After Jessie insisted she wasn't nearly tired enough to stop, Matt took her through the woods along an old riding trail until they had circled the entire eighty acres.

They stopped for a short rest beneath a clump of pine trees. Jessie breathed deeply and then sighed delightedly. She leaned slightly against Matt's side.

"I'm glad this place pleases you," he said.

"I don't know how you can ever leave it."

"It's hard sometimes," Matt admitted, wondering how to move away diplomatically. The tang in the air and the smell of fragrant pines affected him every time he came out here, but combined with Jessie's nearness, the effect was explosive. "It's starting to get dark," Matt said roughly.

When they got back to the house, the sun was nearly hidden behind the trees. "We don't need to go yet, do we?" Jessie asked.

Matt shook his head. "Not if you don't want to. There's some food here if you're hungry."

Jessie was busy putting things together: the mail in the box, the warm breath of the house that could only come from someone living in it, the partially opened windows and dustless tables. "Matt, what is this house to you?"

They stood in the kitchen in the dim glow of twilight. Matt's face was partially hidden in shadow, but Jessie saw the thoughtful look spread across his features. "What is this house to me? That's hard to say. It's a refuge, I guess. I come here to be myself, to be alone." He opened the refrigerator and pulled out a glass casserole dish. It hadn't occurred to him as he spoke that he wasn't alone now, and yet everything else was still in place. There was no discomfort to Jessie's presence.

"It's so lived-in." Jessie sat down on a kitchen chair and braced her elbows on the old oak table. It had the clean scent of oiled furniture and wildflowers. "It doesn't have the feel of a vacation place."

"It's not. I come here a lot, as often as I can. Sometimes during the week I come out just for the night, but weekends are really when I make the most use of it, and summers. This is home to me, not the place in town."

"And the casserole?" She watched him set the dish in the microwave and push some buttons until it began to hum.

"A couple down the road takes care of the property. Helen—she's the wife—cooks for me usually. It works out fine. I don't want anyone living in."

Jessie listened and heard things in between his words. Matt truly was a loner. And he sought it in this wonderful house. There was great irony here, which she knew deserved some attention, but she wasn't at all sure she wanted to grant it. Jessie saw the house differently, not as a solitary haven, but as a warm, joyous home filled with the sounds of laughter, tears and small, running feet. She could imagine children climbing up the branches of the apple trees, playing hide-and-seek in the wonderful, old-smelling attic and sliding down the curved banister with smiles filling their faces. She shook her head slightly as the thoughts took hold.

Matt caught the movement. "What's wrong?"

"Nothing. I was just thinking—about the house, people, how different you and I are."

"The house makes you think that?"

"The house is perfect. But I would never live here alone, that's all."

Matt shrugged. "Each to his own, I guess."

"I would think even the most confirmed bachelor would change his mind and want to marry, fill this house with children."

"Not this one. I'll never have children."

Although Matt's tone was even and unthreatening, Jessie felt shivers ripple up and down her arms. "You're a decisive man."

"About some things." The quiet that settled down on them then was thoughtful, and Matt knew Jessie was sorting through his life in her mind. It didn't bother him. He was what he was. No sense in making excuses. "You, on the other hand, would fill it with kids?"

She nodded. "Dozens."

Matt laughed. "You don't seem to be heading in that direction."

"No, not yet. My day will come. But I work with kids now, over at St. Bede's, so that keeps me connected to them."

"That's the orphanage?"

She nodded.

"Admirable," Matt said.

Jessie looked at him, then spoke thoughtfully. "Not really admirable. It's a give-and-take situation."

"But it must be hard, being with parentless kids."

His voice was strained and Jessie looked at him curiously. She wouldn't have expected Matt to be emotional about the topic. He averted his eyes then and she decided it was her imagination. "Sometimes it's hard," she responded. "Especially with the kids who *have* parents but the parents don't want them, yet they won't give up rights so the kids can be adopted. But that part of it I don't dwell on. There are plenty of experts around St. Bede's to do that. I think about the kids as kids."

Her thoughts turned automatically to her ten-year-old friend Emma, who never strayed too far from her mind. Emma was one of the unadoptables. She had parents somewhere who refused to sign the papers but who hadn't seen Emma since she was three. The little girl was a hemophiliac and her parents had felt cheated, Sister Maria had said. So they left her at St. Bede's and sent a twenty-dollar check on the first of each month. Even when Emma became ill this year, they hadn't come.

Jessie was very attached to the little girl with the huge brown eyes. And Emma's eyes grew larger each time Jessie saw her, because each time there was less of her body, less plumpness to the little girl's cheeks. Her situation was a cruel twist of fate, the result of a life-saving blood transfusion given before screening donated blood for a certain virus became mandatory. The transfusion had betrayed her. AIDS was not being gentle in its ravaging of Emma Hunter.

"Well," Matt said at last, "It's good those kids have friends like you. Now, are you hungry?"

Jessie smiled. "Do you realize how our friendship has been focused on food?"

Matt dished up two heaping plates of a cheesy meat mixture that filled the kitchen with spicy, wonderful smells. "I guess we're trying to satisfy the old appetites in a conventional way," he said. He had meant it as a joke but neither of them laughed.

Jessie stared at the tiny golden rivers of melted cheese on her dish. She knew what was coming—those gentle waves of pleasure that began in the very center of her and moved like thick honey through her body.

"Bad joke," Matt said.

Jessie looked up. Her eyes were a little sad. "No, it wasn't, Matt. It's just us, I guess. Sometimes I feel as if you've drugged me. My blood is full of something that leaps into fire at the slightest suggestion. That's crazy, isn't it?"

She gazed at him with such sincerity that Matt felt she really wanted an answer, wanted him to explain it all away by a chemical formula so the sexual tension between them could then be set aside to dissipate itself—explained, understood and shelved. "It's the damndest thing," was all he replied.

"Well, let's eat." Jessie picked up her fork and smiled brightly. She concentrated on the casserole and vowed to take some books on emotional disorders out of the library as soon as possible.

When Matt dropped her off at her small apartment a few hours later, Jessie wasn't feeling much better. The black sky was empty, with no stars or moon. She stood at her window and watched Matt drive off. The tears that sprang up were confusing.

"Okay, Mayor Ridgefield," she said with little optimism, "I need help with this man. Care to offer any?"

Her apartment was heavy with silence.

Five

———

Emma Hunter's tiny body was nearly hidden in the rose-colored warm-ups she and Jessie had picked out the week before. The little girl sat quietly on a chaise longue on the orphanage sunroof. A small fist supported her chin and her eyes were focused intently on the hills just visible beyond the high protective wall of the roof.

"Hi, Em," Jessie said from the doorway. "I thought I'd find you here. How're things?"

Emma spun around on the chair and looked at the woman she considered to be her best friend in the whole world. "Everything's okay, Jessie. Why are you here?"

Jessie shrugged, then walked over and gave Emma a hug. "I had some business nearby and thought I'd stop in. My friend Marilyn is going to pick me up soon."

"Oh." Emma turned away from Jessie and continued to look out beyond the tops of the buildings. "How far away is that?" She pointed to the hills.

Jessie followed the point of Emma's finger. The hills were the ones near Matt's country house, she remembered, and the memory stirred her. "Not far," she said. "Twenty, thirty miles maybe, as the crow flies. Maybe we'll drive out there some time." Jessie stood near the back of Emma's chair. With her fingers she combed out the tangles in the child's silky brown hair. "So, kiddo, when do you have to be in class?"

Jessie was asking something she already knew; the nuns had told her the answer when she went looking for Emma. The fourth grader's class, taught by the sisters who ran both the orphanage and the hospital next door, had begun thirty minutes ago.

Emma looked at Jessie out of the corner of her eye. "You know."

Jessie nodded. "Yeah, I do. I bet they're missing their smartest kid."

"Maybe," Emma said.

"How are you feeling?"

Emma shrugged a bony shoulder and Jessie noticed that she had lost more weight.

"Still don't have your oomph back, huh?"

"Not yet. But it's coming, I guess."

"Want to go for a walk?"

Emma nodded.

They had to walk down three flights of stairs and Jessie noticed Emma was out of breath. Maybe a walk wasn't such a good idea. She'd lead the child to a bench right away where they could talk.

"So, Emma," Jessie said when the two were settled beneath the spreading branches of an old elm tree on the shady grounds, "what gives with this school stuff?"

"I just didn't want to go, that's all."

"Why?"

"What difference does it make?"

"Maybe not much. Not today, anyway."

"Jessie . . ." Emma's voice was thin.

Jessie wrapped an arm around her shoulders and waited.

"My body makes me mad," Emma said sharply.

"I know," Jessie hugged her tightly.

"Am I pretty, Jessie?" Emma asked suddenly, her eyes widening as they pleaded with Jessie for an answer that would be honest but feel good, too.

Jessie buried her face in Emma's hair. "Oh, sweetie, of course you are. You're beautiful." She straightened and swallowed the lump in her throat. "I think you and I need to have our pictures taken together at Woolworth's and then I can prove to you how pretty you are."

"Okay."

"Would you like an Alexander story?" Jessie asked, deciding on the spot that being together right now was more important than the math class Emma was missing.

Emma's eyes began to smile. "Sure, tell me about Alexander."

For two weeks now Jessie had been dipping into Alexander Ridgefield's life and telling it to her small friends at the orphanage. She supposed the stories came about because, except for Matt, Alexander Ridgefield was the biggest thing on her mind these days and she was actually becoming quite fond of the man who had died some seventy-five years before.

A wind picked up from the north and Jessie pulled Emma into the protection of her arms as she began the latest tale, one that would include the night Alexander spent in jail as a result of mistaken identity.

The laughter that pinked Emma's face at the end was worth gold to Jessie and she had the distinct feeling that Alexander Ridgefield, wherever he was, was also pleased.

"Well, Em," she said, glancing down at her wristwatch, "I guess we better walk back up to the Big Gray."

"I guess so," Emma said, frowning at the stone buildings in the distance. She tucked her small hand inside the soft pocket of her warm-ups and walked alongside Jessie. "But you remember your promise, don't you, Jessie?"

"And when, young lady, have I ever forgotten a promise to you?" Jessie feigned a stern look.

"Never," Emma admitted. "So when?"

"Soon, Em. As soon as you clear up this cough, and Doctor Ned says it's okay, we'll be off like a herd of turtles."

Emma giggled and Jessie looked up so the little girl couldn't see the worried look that shadowed her face. She had promised Emma a whole weekend just for her, away from gray buildings and white coats. Two days to talk and wander and eat pizza and tacos and French fries and anything else they could think of that wasn't healthy. They'd talk about girl things and she'd French-braid Emma's hair and they'd sleep as late in the morning as they wanted to. "Yep," she said aloud, "soon, soon. And now we need to hurry or my friend will leave and you'll have to share your bed with me. And—" she looked down at Emma and squeezed her shoulders "—I snore like crazy."

They rounded a clump of trees and Jessie scanned the circular drive to see if Marilyn's shiny red Saab was waiting. Instead, a dusty Jeep held center court.

Jessie's heart thumped. She took a few steps closer to the familiar vehicle. Yes, it was Matt's. What was he doing here? Her first thought was that he was ill; her second was that he needed her; and her third, calming her heartbeat and bringing order to her bewildered mind, was that people like Matt didn't get sick nor would he probably ever need her. She grabbed Emma's hand and walked over.

Matt's elbow was out the window. He had on his glasses and was reading a thick book propped up on the steering wheel. He was totally immersed in the words in front of him.

"Are you waiting for the light to change?" Jessie asked softly.

Matt looked up slowly, a foggy expression clouding his face as he tried to disentangle himself from eighteenth-century Europe. Then the fog lifted and he smiled at Jessie. "Oh, hello."

Jessie looked down at Emma and Matt followed her gaze. Two lovely brown eyes were staring up at him.

"Emma," Jessie said, "this is my friend."

"Marilyn?" Emma asked.

"No. I don't know where Marilyn is. This is Matt Ridgefield."

"Oh," Emma said. Then her serious face opened up into a cautious smile. "Ridgefield? I know someone by that name. Is he your father?"

Jessie caught a peculiar look on Matt's face at the mention of his father, but it disappeared quickly and he said calmly, "Who do you know, Emma?"

"Alexander Richard Ridgefield. He's our friend!"

Hearing his ancestor's name breathed out with such robust enthusiasm from this small, unexpected source made Matt laugh. "Oh, that Ridgefield," he said. "He was my great-grandfather."

After a quick introduction, Jessie explained about the stories and told Matt that she and Emma had just finished talking about one of them. She wondered what Matt would think of his relative being turned into a children's maverick hero.

"That explains us," Jessie said. "We were telling stories. Now why are you here?"

"I'm here to pick you up. Marilyn said you needed a ride and she had something come up unexpectedly."

"Oh."

"Is that okay? I'm safe, Jess."

What was that supposed to mean, *I'm safe*? Every time Jessie saw Matt these days, she understood him less and wanted him more. That was hardly a safe situation. Out loud she said, "Well, good. Let me run in with Emma and I'll be right out."

Matt looked beyond her to the gray, forbidding building. Then he looked at the pale, beautiful young girl.

"I live here," Emma explained matter-of-factly.

Matt nodded. Because he'd never had much practice, he didn't know how to talk to kids. It had never bothered him before, but today, right now, he had a sudden desire to say something to put a sparkle in the large eyes that watched him so carefully. He couldn't think of a word.

"Come on, kiddo," Jessie said, touching Emma on the shoulder. "We've planned this just right. Class is over."

Emma mustered a smile and said goodbye to Matt. Jessie walked inside with her.

She was back in a minute and slid into the car next to Matt. "Well, what do you think of my friend Emma?"

"She's a beautiful kid," he said.

"She doesn't have family," Jessie explained, even though he hadn't asked. "At least she has none who claim her. She's lived at St. Bede's since she was three." Jessie paused, then went on. "She's been ill for a few months so now she's back and forth between the hospital and the home."

Matt was still, his mind sorting through the information.

"They're good to her here," Jessie said into the silence. "The nuns are, and she loves them. It works out okay."

"How sick is she?"

"She has AIDS."

Jessie waited for Matt to speak but he didn't. He was looking straight ahead, but she knew he was listening, working on what she had said. "Some days aren't so bad for her," Jessie said softly. She found she sometimes glossed over Emma's disease; it made it seem less real and she was never sure of people's responses. She rarely talked about it with others. But suddenly, sitting next to Matt, she found herself wanting to talk about it, and without conscious intent, the words poured forth. She told him about Emma's diagnosis, about her hatred of this evil that had fallen on an innocent young girl, of how much she loved Emma. She told him about the bout of pneumonia Emma had already been through, and how her whole small body shook when she coughed. She told him how she feared Emma's death.

Matt's stomach constricted. His hands gripped the wheel until his knuckles turned white.

Jessie was silent for a long time. When she spoke again, her voice was calmer. "But Emma's remarkable, Matt," she said. "I've known her for a long time, from long before she became sick. And I don't know, she seems to know things I don't sometimes. She sees things in life that require a wisdom far beyond her years."

Matt drove away from the hospital. He listened to Jessie carefully but kept silent. His mind was tortured with inconsistencies. The face of the little girl stayed with him as he drove, and he thought about her life, her *short*, interrupted life, and the fact that she had no choice in the matter. Some people did have that choice, and they ended their lives. "It doesn't make a helluva lot of sense, does it?" he finally said. His voice was strained and angry.

"No," Jessie said. "It doesn't. But life often doesn't make sense." She looked out over the river as they crossed the bridge marking the center of town. The water was moving today and in the distance she could see a small sailboat weaving its way in from the open sea. Out there it was quiet and peaceful. She turned back to Matt. "It's too late to go back to the office. Would you mind just dropping me at my apartment?"

"Whatever you want."

"I suppose you're lecturing tonight."

"No, not tonight."

"Oh."

Jessie nibbled on her bottom lip. Matt was her friend; one could ask things of friends, even though said friend was sometimes as distant as Mars. Friends helped each other. Jessie pulled her brows together and her mind charged on. Friends met needs, and tonight, right now, she had some needs. Jessie didn't want to go back to her apartment at all; she wanted to be with a friend.

"On second thought," Jessie said out loud, "I don't really want to go back to my apartment. My refrigerator has one bruised apple and a cup of yogurt with dark green fuzz on the top of it. Would you have dinner with me?"

Matt continued to look ahead at the gray serpentine road. The idea had crossed his mind. Ideas, in fact, that involved more than dinner, which was why he'd kept silent.

His thoughts of Jessie sometimes came at odd unexpected moments—in the middle of a student's recitation on the Spanish Civil War or as he walked across campus and the leaves fell like burnished snowflakes on his jacket and hair. Sometimes the thoughts were as expected and regular as clockwork—like each evening when he stepped out onto the small apartment patio where he had a nightcap and a smoke before bed. Always then. Right now, sitting behind the wheel with her at his side, he was thinking about her and happy that he didn't have to drop her off.

"Well, Matt," Jessie said, "what do you say? I'll treat."

"Hmm—" he replied.

"Okay, okay," Jessie persisted, "dessert, too. Your choice."

"That's hard to turn down."

"So don't."

It was settled, and Jessie felt a surge of happiness that made her sigh deep down inside of herself. She didn't care where they ate—Wendy's, the college cafeteria, or the Rooftop Hyatt. All that mattered was that she be with someone she cared about. She knew seeing Emma today was part of this mood she was in. The child's illness had become a commanding force in Jessie's life, but there were times, like tonight, when she didn't want to be alone with all those horrible facts about Emma's disease that tore at her insides and left her feeling limp and helpless.

"How's this?" Matt asked. He pulled the Jeep into a parking lot next to a shake-shingled building with large expanses of glass on one side. It was a small, intimate restaurant on the river bend and it commanded views of the water as it widened out toward the sea. The sun had disappeared completely and fat, gray clouds were filling the sky.

"It's perfect," Jessie said. She wanted to touch Matt, to have his presence be an integral part of her, but instead she merely walked close beside him as they went inside. They followed the maître d' to a table by the window and she smiled over at Matt when he sat down across from her. "This is exactly what I needed tonight. Exactly."

The dining room was casual and delicious aromas mingled with the outside smells of the sea. Jessie sighed, sat back in her chair and closed her eyes.

"You're not going to go to sleep on me, are you?"

Jessie slowly raised her lids. "No. I was just relaxing, settling the day."

"Would you like some wine?" Matt summoned the waiter who came over immediately and hovered at his elbow.

Jessie shook her head. "But you go ahead. I don't drink."

Matt ordered a glass of wine, added a Perrier for Jessie, and then turned his attention back to her. "Is it on moral or religious grounds, or do you simply not like liquor?"

"Not religious, but maybe the other two."

Matt lifted his brows.

"No," she said quickly, "I don't mean it's immoral for you to drink. But it might be for me. Genes, you see."

Matt remembered then. Jessie's father had been a drunk, and the remnants of his harmful addiction were woven into the look in Jessie's eyes. "Your dad," he said. "I'd forgotten."

Jessie nodded. "Who knows? I might be a fine social drinker, but why chance it? And besides, the memories of what liquor did to my family make it an absurd option for me."

Matt heard the pain in her voice and again he felt the angry constriction in his chest. Her father had ruined her childhood, just as his own father had ruined his. As he was about to say something about the cruel hands life can deal a kid, Jessie smiled and continued talking.

"You know," she said, "it has its good points, living with someone like my father. There's no burden of living up to whatever he was, or whatever his expectations of me might have been. He didn't have any.'' She laughed lightly at the end of the sentence, the kind of laugh that closes off the thought, rather than indicating enjoyment.

Matt mused about that but didn't respond. He thought of his own father, of the effort he had put into burying his memory. But it was there, staring at him. The man he had loved so deeply, and who had betrayed him with the most severe betrayal of all. When he looked up, Jessie was smiling at him and the memory began to blur. He sat back in the chair and looked at her thoughtfully. ''The thing about your situation, though, is that you had no choice. Your father was a certain way, and you suffered for it. That's unfair to you.''

Jessie shrugged. ''What monopoly do I have on things like that? You work with the life you're given.''

''But your choices were limited by your father, not by anything you did.'' His fingers drummed on the table-cloth.

''Most people's choices are limited by others, Matt. Even loving someone can limit choices.'' Jessie was looking at Matt curiously now because he seemed to want to say more than he was. He looked pained by what he was asserting, and Jessie didn't understand it at all.

''Sorry, Jess,'' he murmured abruptly. ''I got carried away. You seem to have handled your family situation just fine.''

''Oh, I don't know about that. I just don't let my past dictate my future. And I wasn't Little Orphan Annie or anything, even though I didn't *like* huge parts of my childhood. But—'' She paused, stopped by the feeling that this conversation had gone on long enough. She didn't like dwelling on the past, and Matt seemed unhappy with it as well. She looked at him intently, then broke into a grin that lit up the table. "But as I see it, Professor Ridgefield, *good* things come along too, things I never expected or chose. Like you, for instance." She reached out and touched the back of his hand. "I'm awfully glad I found you. I will be forever grateful to my obsession for bagels."

The light pressure of her fingers burned on the back of his hand, but Matt held himself still. He buried the old feelings that had attacked him with an unexpected vengeance, and instead he concentrated on the woman in front of him. "I take the credit for this one, Jessie," he said. "I found you."

She smiled again and withdrew her hand. "Kismet," she explained.

The meal was wonderful—heaping plates of fresh crab legs, shrimp and crisp vegetables that Matt and Jessie consumed eagerly. Matt marveled silently at the effect Jessie had on his appetite. It was sharper, stronger, and food smelled better. Another irrational side effect of Jessie Sager. He took a sip of coffee and looked across the table. Jessie was absorbed in her dessert, a rich chocolate concoction that was bringing her great delight.

"Marilyn says the book is coming along fine," he said.

She agreed. "And I love it. It certainly beats writing about the grand opening of another delicatessen or the annual Little Miss Contest. I think this job is really tapping my soul, Matt." Her enthusiasm made her brown eyes glow.

"Good."

"I'm learning fascinating things about the Ridgefields, too," she admitted. "Which is nice, because you don't tell me much."

Matt stiffened but Jessie didn't seem to notice and she continued.

"Alexander's son Hamilton—your grandfather—was almost as interesting as his father."

"Maybe, but why does he matter? He's not the subject of the book."

"Matt Ridgefield, you'd almost think you were ashamed of your relatives. Of course it matters, he was the mayor's only son, after all." Jessie took a final forkful of her dessert and pushed the plate away. "He was very much like his father—bright, ambitious, successful." Jessie knew from the look on Matt's face that she was pushing now. But she didn't understand his silence on the Ridgefield men. They were wildly successful forefathers of the whole Manchester area. Hamilton had founded a successful lumber company that had provided work for half the county, and the other half he employed on his development projects. As Jessie devoured the history of these aggressive men, she sometimes wondered about Matt's low profile, his totally different life-style. And she was quite curious. "I even came across a picture of you on your grandfather's lap at a town meeting. The reporter labeled the picture 'Hamilton Ridgefield and His Right Hand Man.'"

"I've seen it. Would you like some coffee?"

"No, thanks."

"Then maybe we should leave." Matt looked across the room and summoned the waiter for the check without waiting for a reply.

Jessie drew her brows together, absolutely mystified over his change of mood. She snapped the check from his hand. "My treat, remember?"

"Don't be silly," Matt started.

"I'm not silly. But you're certainly moody." Jessie snapped open her purse and counted out the bills.

"Sorry about that" was all he said as he held open the door and they both stepped out of the restaurant into a fine mist.

Jessie found the rain a welcome diversion. She hugged her sweater to her body and looked up into the black sky. Light drops fell on her face. Matt took her arm. "Let's go. You'll get soaked."

Jessie pulled away and continued to welcome the water on her face. "It's not raining hard. And it's a beautiful night. Let's walk down to the river."

"You're daffy, Jess."

"And full, too. I need to walk some of this off." And she also needed to put behind them the mood that she had inadvertently drawn out of Matt. She urged him toward the brick pathway that led down to a pier.

Matt wiped some moisture from his forehead and followed her quietly. He wanted to erase the mood, too. Jessie's curiosity was certainly natural, but his family ties were buried, not something he wanted to talk about with anyone, not even Jessie.

They wandered silently out to the end of the short dock. All around them were the soothing sounds of the gentle rain hitting the water and the slow swaying of tree branches at the river's edge. Two dim gaslights flickered off the surface of the river.

They stood together, their arms looped comfortably around one another. Beyond them the night sky stretched out into the eternal blackness and the rain dutifully washed away the discord.

"There," Jessie said, smiling up into his shadowed face. "Feel better?"

"I didn't feel bad."

"Just grumpy, then. I'm sorry."

"No need to be."

Jessie shifted and her body rubbed nicely against Matt's hip.

Damn, Matt thought. There was only so much a man could take. He tried to stay away from Jessie, but everything conspired the other way. She pressed closer to him and he inhaled the clean smell of rain in her hair. Everything about her was an aphrodisiac.

The discomfort over Jessie stepping into his past wasn't entirely gone, but the edge of irritation did nothing to blur the feelings of arousal. He should have anticipated it—standing alone with her like this in the darkness. Jessie moved her head then and her damp hair brushed his cheek.

Slowly Matt turned her body toward him until her back was to the river and the misty lights at the edge of the dock flickered across her damp skin. Her cheeks glistened as she looked up at him and raindrops clung to her eyelids. She smiled.

"Jessie, I—"

"Me, too, so let's." She raised herself up on tiptoe and the slight movement brought Matt's head down to meet her open lips. Their kiss was soft, full of the feeling of the evening. And then it grew more urgent, and Matt nipped gently, drinking the rainwater from her skin. He tasted the rich pleasure of her mouth, pulling her closer to him until he felt he was going to explode.

But the explosion came from another source far above them. Clouds broke open completely and a sudden torrent replaced the light, pleasing drizzle and forced their bodies apart.

"Oh, hell!" Matt yelled above the storm sounds, and he grabbed Jessie's hand. Together they tore up the incline and raced to his Jeep.

"I guess that's one way to take a cold shower," Matt said as they drove off. He'd turned the heat up and given

Jessie a blanket from the back seat to soak up some of the water.

"Yeah," murmured Jessie, lost in her own thoughts. There was a space between them on the seat but she could still feel the physical contact with him. The power of his kiss was overwhelming. She'd never felt this way with anyone else, not the deep, racing emotion that passed between them when they touched. She wanted to think about it, explore it, try to figure it out.

"I'm not sure what's going on here, Matt," she said when Matt pulled up in front of her apartment.

Matt touched her cheek lightly with two fingers. "I don't either. I don't want to hurt you, Jessie."

"Then don't."

"Life's simple for you, isn't it?"

"No, life has never been simple for me. And you're not simple. But we mean something to each other. I don't know for sure what. But it's going to be harder to keep ignoring it, don't you think?"

His eyes explored her face. "Yeah," he said finally. "It's going to be hard to ignore it. But sometimes the harder way's the better. In the end, I mean."

"You're pontificating, Professor, and not making a lot of sense. Maybe you need to simplify your thoughts a little. Adopt some of the philosophy Emma's had to live with. You know, sometimes all we have is today."

Jessie could see the struggle in Matt's eyes. She started to shiver then and she knew she'd better get out of the car fast. She needed either a hot bath to warm her body or Matt's arms. And something inside her told her the hot bath would be easier to leave. At least for tonight.

Six

___

When Matt told her the next day that he was attending an educational conference in Boston for a few days, Jessie was almost relieved, and Matt seemed to be of the same opinion. His presence was such a jolting force these days that a short hiatus might draw her back into feeling normal.

She was doing a dance with Matt that he seemed to be leading, a moving together, then a pulling away. But each time he pulled away, he left a little more of himself inside her.

Yes, Jessie decided, as she threw herself into researching the Ridgefield manuscript, absence would create clear thinking. She ignored any thoughts about the heart growing fonder.

"What in heaven's name are you doing here?" Marilyn asked as she strode into Jessie's office early Saturday morning.

"Umph," Jessie said, trying to lift her head from the cluttered desktop. Her hair wisped haphazardly around her face and there was a red crease across her cheek where it had rested on a pencil.

"Jessie, answer me."

Jessie pried open her eyes and tried to smile.

"Have you been here all night?"

"If it's morning, I guess so. It was dark last time I looked." She propped her head up with her hands and grinned crookedly.

"Ridiculous. This isn't your whole life, you know. And you're far ahead of where we'd be without you."

"I didn't intend to stay all night. I decided to rest my eyes for a minute before going home."

"I guess you did." Marilyn walked over and rubbed her shoulders lightly.

Jessie sighed. "That feels great, Marilyn."

"And I have another treat for you, my friend." She dropped a bulging file on the desk in front of Jessie. "Ed Wiley over at the *Daily News* had an intern copy all these articles for us on the Ridgefields. The youngster was a little overzealous—it looks like he pulled anything that even mentioned the name Ridgefield. You might have to do a little sorting."

"That's okay. Thanks. I needed these clippings to do the last leg of that draft—"

"On Monday."

Jessie forked her fingers through her hair. "You're probably right. Although this desk *is* amazingly comfortable. I slept like a baby."

Marilyn laughed. "You must have one peculiar mattress at home."

"Maybe." Jessie flipped open the file and leafed absently through the copies.

Marilyn started toward the door. "I have to leave, Jessie. When you venture out, you'll find a gorgeous day out there. Go take a look at it and—"

"Smell the roses, right?" Jessie stretched back in the chair and smiled at her friend. Marilyn was right. A breather would help her work even faster on Monday. A breather... Her thoughts slid from work to Matt and she knew taking a breather meant seeing him. The week apart had made her miss him dreadfully. And absence didn't do a thing to calm the desire he'd unleashed in her. If this wasn't meant to be, it was going to take something other than absence to dampen her ardor. Maybe talking to him would help. But whether it did or not, she needed to see him as surely as a starving person needed food.

"Jessie, are you listening?" Marilyn looked at her sternly from the door.

"Aye, aye, sir," Jessie said, pulling herself up straight. "I promise to leave soon. I'm going to take a few minutes to organize this stuff so it's ready to zip through on Monday and then I'm out of here. Maybe I'll call Matt."

"He's not around. I ran into him yesterday—"

"Yesterday?" Jessie didn't know he was back and she pushed away the slight hurt that welled inside.

Marilyn nodded. "He said he was on his way out to that place of his in the country—his hermitage. He seemed tired."

Jessie looked out the window. He'd been in the country in last night's dream, too. So had she. Her hand lifted to cover the heat she felt rising to her cheeks. "Oh" was all she spoke out loud.

"Well, I'll be going," Marilyn said, wondering at the peculiar expression that crossed Jessie's face.

Jessie pushed a lively smile into place. "See you Monday. Oh, and thanks." She lifted the file.

Marilyn nodded and left, throwing a final warning to Jessie not to waste her youth on work. Jessie smiled after her, then sat back in the chair, suddenly engulfed in a sea of loneliness. It was strange, she thought absently, for she wasn't a lonely person. But suddenly she was, right now, on this beautiful fall day.

Matt was in the country.

He hadn't taken her out there since that first time, nor had he even suggested it. She had felt so close to him that day, and she suspected that was part of the problem for Matt. Their easy friendship had disappeared too readily in the tranquil seclusion of his wooded home. As naturally as breathing, their friendship had swelled with the stirrings of passion, and that was why Matt was keeping her away.

She leafed through the clippings, wondering about him and about her life. It was different now, with Matt in it, and she was finding it more and more difficult to imagine her life without him. Nor did she want to, and that was disturbing. She didn't want Matt to be a walk-through, and she considered how much longer they could play this buddy game. She shook her head, pushed away the discomforting feelings and concentrated on the news clippings in her hand.

A bold headline across the top of one of the sheets caught her eye.

Tragedy on Ridgefield Estate, it read.

The headline pierced through Jessie's thoughts and she dropped the rest of the stack on her desk. There was a picture with the article, a photo of a handsome couple. She had seen the two people somewhere before. Jessie looked more closely at the black-and-white print. It was the woman's smile she recognized first. The same smile she had seen in the photo in Matt's office. Matt's mother. There wasn't a child in this picture, but Jessie knew she wasn't mistaken. This photo was of Matt's mother and father.

Her glance slid to the accompanying article, and with a feeling of foreboding, Jessie read on:

Businessman Arthur Matthew Ridgefield, 38, and his wife Katherine Marie Ridgefield, died early Tuesday morning. According to Sam Whitmann, county coroner, Mr. and Mrs. Ridgefield each died of a single bullet wound. Allegedly, Ridgefield shot his wife while she slept in her bed, and then killed himself....

Jessie dropped the clipping on the desk. Her mind was blank and her head filled with a rush of emotion that made her feel faint. Suicide . . . Both his parents dead.

She picked up the article again, but it was some time before her eyes could focus on the black type. A terrible sadness began to seep into her. She read to the bottom of the page and then the words blurred before her eyes. Jessie lowered her head to the desk, then salty tears fell freely onto the smooth sheet of paper.

"What are you doing here?" Matt stood in the doorway of the house, his brows pulled together in a frown. He was utterly surprised to see Jessie standing there. Sometimes on Saturday delivery people from the town dropped things off, but Jessie was the last person he had expected to see.

"Hello, Matt," Jessie said quietly. "May I come in?"

Matt looked over her shoulder at a small Honda parked in the drive.

"I borrowed it from Mr. Bourke. It's his daughter's," Jessie replied in answer to his puzzled look.

"Borrowed it?"

"You thought maybe I stole it?" Jessie's lips pulled up into a half smile.

Matt didn't answer. He stood quietly, his face a careful mask.

"Hey, fella," Jessie continued lightly, "if you don't let me in after I did something as crazy as borrowing my boss's car—I don't drive much, you see, so this is a risky venture—you may not like the consequences. An angry Jessie is an awesome thing."

Matt gazed into her incredibly soft eyes. He was angry with her. Why did she look at him like that? She was uprooting his resolutions, invading his turf, doing damnable things to his libido. Roughly, he pulled her into the hallway and stood there, his hands on her shoulders, his eyes on her calm, determined face. She was so beautiful, so sexy, so—

"Do you have any coffee?"

"You came all the way out here for coffee?" He didn't know whether to shake her or carry her off to bed. She had no right to come to him like this, to unnerve him, to bring her sweet sexuality into his house and send his blood rushing like the Colorado River through his veins.

"Nope," Jessie said. "You're angry, aren't you?"

Matt softened. He dropped his hands from her shoulder and walked through the hallway into the sun-drenched kitchen. Jessie shoved her hands into her jeans pockets and followed. The sadness that had been the compelling force on the ride to Matt's home had been pushed into the background when she saw him standing on the doorstep. His presence filled her with a jarring emotion. This was the other Matt again, the one with blue jeans covering his solid thighs and a soft flannel shirt pulled across his upper body. His strong jaw was shadowed with a day's growth of beard. His eyes were pensive, lacking the intensity they carried at the college. Even his stance was different, the strength of his body more relaxed, more natural out here in the clean country.

Matt handed her a cup of coffee. "In here." He motioned toward the easy, comfortable family room off the kitchen. French doors and elongated windows pulled the sweet smell of the fields and the pine trees into the room. Jessie settled herself immediately on the oversized sofa, kicking off her shoes and tucking her feet beneath her in the way Matt was coming to expect. "You make decent coffee, Matt," she said. "Not as good as mine, but decent."

"Thank you." Matt sat down in a leather chair opposite her, carefully avoiding the space she had left beside her. "Okay Jess, tell me, to what do I owe this visit?"

Jessie frowned. "Such formality. You sound like a B movie."

"Why are you here, Jessie?"

"Because Marilyn kicked me out of my office, insisted I enjoy the weather, and..."

"And?"

"And I couldn't find anyone else to play with," she finished lamely.

"I see." Matt stretched his feet out in front of him and clasped his hands behind his head. "So you came to play with me?"

"I came to see you. Friends visit friends all the time, Matt." Why had she come? Now she was beginning to wonder. What had she intended to say to him—Matt, I'm so sorry your father killed himself? No, she had come because she cared about him, and hearing of what he had suffered all those years ago had pulled her to him as if the incident had happened yesterday. She suspected that the pain was still there inside him, bottled up, pressing against him. And she thought she understood him better now, even though the disclosure had opened up a million new questions as well.

"There's more to it than that," Matt said. If she had come to seduce him, Matt thought, she was going to be disappointed. He'd worked all that out while he was in Boston. He'd made selfish decisions in his life but he was sure as hell not going to hurt Jessie Sager with one.

Jessie looked at Matt directly. "Yes, there is more to it. There's a whole bunch of reasons why I want to be with you, but only one that brought me today."

Matt sat forward in the chair, his arms resting on his elbows. The look on Jessie's face was too serious to deal with. Whatever it was could wait. She was here, and no matter what his mind told him, his body said that it was a good thing, so he might as well give in to the forces that be and enjoy the afternoon. "Okay, fair enough. I suppose in good time you'll let me in on whatever it is. In the meantime, I was about to check out some things around here. Want to help?"

Jessie unfolded herself immediately and hopped up. "Great! I need some exercise. Put me to work." She was with him, that was enough for now.

First on Matt's list was fixing a broken stile on a fence that bordered one edge of the property. To get to it, they climbed into a small red pickup and bumped their way across the fields.

The wind caught Matt's hair and lifted it off his forehead as he drove. Jessie found the movement entrancing. "This is a great old truck," she said presently.

"Yeah," he agreed. "It's almost as old as I am."

"A real antique, huh?" she commented smugly and Matt laughed. Whatever had been eating at him when she arrived was clearly gone now, Jessie decided, and she was grateful for that, whatever the cause had been. She was grateful to be here, to be with him, to have that awful pang of loneliness erased. His hand had come down on her knee when they bounced over a rut in the field and he kept it there now. Jessie looked down and watched it, liking it there.

When they arrived at the fence, Matt jumped out and lifted a tool kit from behind his seat. "Okay, Jess, your job is to hold while I hammer."

"Sounds easy enough."

The woods came right up to the fence at this spot; some of the new pines hugged the weathered stiles. Jessie stood with her hand on the top of the fence and absorbed the sounds and smells. She picked up a new sound. "Matt, what's that?" She listened again and heard the faint tinkle of water.

Matt came up beside her. "That's the spring. It feeds Rainbow Creek."

In a flash Jessie was over the fence and making her way through the thicket of trees toward the sound. She edged around a stand of half-grown pines and came into the clearing. In the center was a bubbling, icy spring. The clear water pushed its way upward through a bed of pebbles and flowed down a nature-carved path. Branches hung low over the water as if bending down for cool refreshment. Jessie crouched down on the soft, cushiony bank and dipped her hand into the water. The moist, rich smell of pine needles and crushed leaves came up to meet her. "It's cold," she said, knowing without looking that Matt stood just behind her. "May I drink from it?"

"Not until you make a wish," he replied, bending down beside her. "It's said that all wishes at this spring come true, so be careful."

"All right." Jessie put her head back and closed her eyes tightly, her mind sorting through wish possibilities. Finally she opened her eyes and looked up into Matt's. "Okay," she announced, an enigmatic smile flitting across her face. Then she bent over the water, cupped her hands and drank from the clear, cool stream.

Matt watched her closely. The expression on her face brought all sorts of his own wishes to mind. No, not wishes, he thought. Fantasies. And those were safe.

"Well," Matt said when she was finished, "here's to wishes. May yours come true." He, too, drank the spring water while Jessie tucked away his words. Yes, she felt suddenly. It would come true. The feelings had grown so naturally in her that there was no one moment she would be able to point to, but today, kneeling by the creek and feeling the clear, cold water slide down her throat, was the first time she had put those feelings into a clear thought: she loved Matt Ridgefield.

"Are you ready to work now?" Matt asked, standing tall beside her.

Jessie swallowed the lump in her throat and got up. It was then she spotted the wild daisies covering the gentle slope of earth on the other side of the creek. She loved daisies, and it was significant, she thought, that she spotted them now. Their yellow faces were pushed flat open against the brown and green of the brush behind them and they seemed to celebrate her insight.

"Come on, Jess." Matt turned back onto the fresh path they had made into the woods. "There isn't much daylight left."

"In a second," Jessie said, but her words were muffled by movement as she stepped gingerly onto a flat rock to get across the narrow stream. Two long stretches of leg would have done it if the second crossing stone hadn't been covered with sleek, slippery moss.

Matt looked back over his shoulder just as Jessie's tennis shoe began to slide across the stone's surface. Before what was happening registered in his mind, Jessie's arms were waving frantically in the air, her body bending back and forth as it desperately sought a balance. And then with the same grace with which Matt had seen her toss a doll in an oven and slide across a stage on her bottom, she landed on the pebbled bottom of Rainbow Creek. Icy water closed in around her.

She was okay, Matt could see that readily from the crooked smile that slipped slowly across her face.

"Darn," she said lamely.

"Yeah," Matt murmured. "You do the damndest things." He was beside her now and carefully lifted her limp, wet form from the creek bed. She looked defenseless, small and fragile, and Matt restrained himself so he wouldn't crush her in his arms.

"No. I just wanted a daisy, that's all," she said softly. With Matt's arms supporting her, she rose and stepped gingerly onto the hard ground. Water squished noisily out of her tennis shoes. "So much for pirouetting across streams."

"But you fall so gracefully."

"Practice, my dear Professor, that's all." She let him pull her close into the warmth of his body. The icy cold of the stream was now in her blood, coursing through her arms and legs.

"Jess, you're shivering."

"It's all a grand scheme to get out of work." Her teeth chattered when she spoke. "I think I want to go home, Matt."

Matt bundled Jessie in a thick blanket he kept in the back of the truck and by the time the final rays of the sun slipped beyond the hills, they were back at the house. Only when he had Jessie inside and up in his bedroom did it occur to Matt that not only had Jessie referred to his house as "home," but that it sounded right.

Matt insisted on her taking a hot bath and Jessie didn't argue much. It was too hard to talk through her blue, numb lips. She closed the door, peeled off her soaked clothes and slipped slowly into the tub, breathing in the steam as it rose from the sudsy water. Her body sank beneath the surface until only her head remained above and she sighed from the pure pleasure of it. As warmth began to return to her body, she rested her head against the back of the tub and looked around.

The bathroom was old but fitted with lovely new fixtures, elegant things, really, like the whirlpool tub that had room for Jessie and a friend or two. She shoved *that* thought out of her mind immediately, concentrating instead on the colors reflecting on the bubbles. It was surely enough she was alone with Matt in his home, alone and naked! She didn't need her mind to go off on one of its erotic binges.

Jessie closed her eyes. Soft music came from somewhere far off and it washed over her like the soap and the hot water and the steamy air. She felt herself floating, dreaming. Against all good sense and training, she let her imagination loose to explore the forbidden: Matt entering the plush bathroom, his jeans riding low on his hips, his moody smile replaced with the sexy look she caught him wearing at odd moments. He'd walk all the way over to the edge of the tub and look down at her. She'd smile back—shyly, of course—and he'd dip a crooked finger into the bath, catching a weightless puff of bubbles and blowing it into the air. Then he'd sit on the side, his eyes on her face first, then slowly lowering to her breasts. They'd be pink and glistening from the soapy water. She would slide down a bit into the water, and he'd laugh huskily at her modesty, and when she had turned her head for a half moment to lift a bar of soap from the shell-shaped holder, Matt would shed his jeans and shirt and slip into the large oval tub. His body would be slippery and smooth next to hers, and—

"Jessie?"

Jessie's heart lurched, and then it seemed to sink directly to the bottom of the enormous tub, pulling her along with it until her mouth stung with fragrant soap.

"Jessie, are you all right?"

All right? A drowned nymphomaniac, that's what she was, but all right? Of course not! She groped along the edge of the tub until her fingers felt an enormous towel. She mopped the water from her face and eyes, and then she found her voice. "I'm fine, Matt," she said. "The water's wet."

"Yes," Matt replied. "I like it that way."

"Oh." A pause. "I'll be out in a minute."

"No hurry. It was so quiet, I thought maybe you'd gone to sleep."

"Ha," Jessie said.

"Well, I guess I'd better leave you alone. There's a fire downstairs."

Jessie heard his footsteps disappear along the hall and she sat up straight in the tub, scrubbing her hair. Then she pulled herself out of the tub and walked resolutely into the blue-tiled, glass-enclosed shower, where she stood tall and refused to wince when the cold spray of water bombarded her body.

"It looks good on you," Matt said when Jessie padded into the family room, her body wrapped in the thick, fleecy robe Matt had left for her on his bed.

He was standing in front of the fireplace holding a drink and looking far more pensive than Jessie thought he should. Was it because she was here? "It was considerate of you to leave it for me. My clothes seemed to have disappeared."

"They're in the dryer."

He was watching her carefully and Jessie felt strangely unnerved. "Well, thanks," she said. "As soon as they're done I'll be off."

"No," Matt countered simply.

Jessie glanced out the window. Beyond the thick panes of glass it was pitch black.

"You can't drive these roads in the dark if you're not familiar with them. You'll have to stay."

Jessie sat down on the couch. She was starting to shiver again. It was a stranger talking to her, not the Matt in whom she'd invested her wish at the stream. "Matt, I—"

"I've got some steaks ready to go when you're hungry."

Jessie lifted her head and saw a flicker of gentleness in his eyes. No, she was wrong. It was the same Matt, but this was the side of him that eluded her, the side that tried to hold her at a distance. She thought back to the newspaper clippings, to his parents, to that chapter in Matt's life that had stared out at her so boldly just hours before. They were connected, she knew, this dark mood and the tragedy that had been inflicted on him in his youth. It was all real, like a third person imposing himself between them. Jessie's own past did that sometimes—reared its head and made her afraid, but the present was too precious, the future too exciting for her to allow the past to control her. So she forced it away, out of her mind and heart, and went on living. She wasn't so sure about Matt.

"Would you like a glass of sherry?" he was asking from where he stood. "It'll help take away the chill."

"Hot tea would be nice."

Matt returned minutes later with the tea and this time he surprised Jessie and himself by sitting down on the couch next to her. He'd made a list of resolutions while she was in the bath; it was one way of keeping himself busy so he wouldn't dwell on the fact that she was in his bathroom, naked and beautiful. He had concentrated instead, as best he could, on what should and shouldn't be. And it came down to one thing—that he, Matt Ridgefield, had no right becoming romantically involved with Jessie Sager. It was as clear to him as anything had ever been in his life.

What wasn't so clear was how to handle it when she showed up on his doorstep and settled down in his living room wrapped in his robe, flushed and beautiful and desirable. She was pressing all the strategic buttons. There was just so much a man could take....

"Matt, I—"

"Jessie—"

Their words collided in the fire-heated air. Simultaneous tentative laughter followed.

"I'll go first," Jessie said, setting her cup down on the coffee table and resting a hand on Matt's leg. "I'm sorry I barged in on your weekend, Matt. I didn't think before I came and I can see I've made a mess of things."

"Certainly not a mess. I'm not used to guests, that's all. My social graces are a little rusty."

Jessie looked into the fire. Finally she faced Matt again. "No, I don't care about social graces. It's something else. I hadn't been able to figure you out, Matt. I would feel close to you, and then shut out. Sometimes you try to be a stranger to me, but I know you don't feel that way. It's been confusing.''

Matt took a long drink of the Scotch and soda he'd been nursing. If she'd remove her hand from his thigh he knew he'd be able to think more clearly. ''I'm not sure this is the place or time to talk about this, Jessie. You must be hungry.''

Jessie smiled. ''For once in my life I'm not. Matt, I did some heavy-duty thinking on the way up here—''

''Well, I don't think—''

''Wait, Matt.'' Her fingers held his thigh tighter. ''Just keep quiet for a while.''

Matt forgot for a minute that people didn't usually talk to him that way. Maybe it was the sad desperation in her voice. He stopped talking.

''I think I know what's going on here.'' Jessie took a deep breath and plunged in. ''You like me, Matt Ridgefield. You like me a hell of a lot. You're attracted to me. There's a...a karma at work here.''

''A karma?''

''Yes,'' Jessie said, undaunted. He wasn't going to stop her now. ''It's there, as plain as the hair on your chest. Your *head*! But relationships scare you.''

He scowled at her. It didn't block out the sensations traveling from the tips of her fingers on his thigh to parts he didn't care to think about right now.

''And I finally understand why,'' Jessie continued.

The scowl disappeared. Mild amusement replaced it.

''Matt, I know how your parents died.''

Matt didn't move, but all the pleasurable sensations died in an instant.

''I came across some clippings. Accidentally, Matt. I wasn't prying.'' She searched his face but it was unreadable. His jaw was set firmly and there wasn't any light spilling from his eyes. She shifted on the couch and turned so she was facing him fully. "I can understand some things now, Matt—"

"Oh, you can?"

His voice was cool, professorial. Someone she didn't know was talking. Jessie shivered, but she went on.

"Both of us had less than ideal families, it looks like."

"You might say that."

"But I think yours still lives with you."

"Mine is buried, Jessie."

"But the pain of it, what your father did—"

"My father killed himself, Jessie, because *his* father insisted he succeed in the family business. And when my father's company began to fail, he turned from a loving, kind man into a desperate man. You see, failure wasn't acceptable. My grandfather wasn't satisfied with the emotional torture my father was going through; he needed to bring the lesson home. So he wrote my parents out of his will and left his fortune—a sizeable fortune, I might add—to his grandson."

The newspaper picture of Matt on his grandfather's lap loomed large in Jessie's mind. "To you—" Jessie squeezed her brows together. Her head hurt.

Matt laughed, a cruel, sharp sound. "To me. I'm very rich, Jessie. My grandfather had seen I'd know what to do with the money. I had all the business know-how."

So you probably invested the money and then became a professor, Jessie thought. Of course, it made sense now. You got as far away from that painful world as you could.

Matt continued, his voice pained and matter-of-fact at once.

"My grandfather, whom I'd loved a great deal, demanded things from my father that he was incapable of delivering, and it destroyed him. And my father, whom I'd loved even more, finished it off by failing completely. He gave up. He knew how much my mother depended on him. She wouldn't have been able to handle it. So he took her life, too. I guess he thought I'd be all right. I was seventeen and soon to be a very rich man, so I was spared."

Jessie felt a pain so sharp she couldn't speak.

Matt looked at Jessie. She had had no right to dig all this up. His past was his own private little hell and he dealt with it just fine. But his anger toward her came in ebbs and tides. Uncertain anger.

Jessie's hand rose to his arm. "You're terribly angry with me." She sought his eyes. "Matt, I found out about this accidentally, but I came to you on purpose, because I care about you so much. What has happened to you in the past is a part of you, so I care about that, too. Matt, I—" *Love you.* The words stopped in her throat, huge and choking. But she couldn't say them. Not now. She'd trespassed all over his life already. She couldn't burden him now with her love and she sensed instinctively that that's what it would be.

Matt took a deep breath and released it slowly. When he spoke again his voice was softer. He knew she cared; maybe that's why he was angry, but of course he couldn't tell her that. Prying, meddling he could handle. This was something else. This was disconcerting, this strengthening of the link between them that was making mincemeat out of two decades' worth of hard resolutions. "Jess, I'm not angry," he said carefully, "but what's past is past. And there isn't any possible good in rehashing something that happened over twenty years ago. I've dealt with it."

But how? Jessie wanted to ask. By keeping those who might love you on the other side of the world so you couldn't possibly let them down or fail them the way the young Matt was failed? But she didn't ask him. Instead she wrapped her arms around him, and so he couldn't see the tears in her eyes, she buried her face beneath his chin.

"Jessie, I—" The words dropped off. His arms moved around her, the terry-cloth robe bunched beneath his hands.

"Shh," she said into the heat of his chest. "Just hold me, okay?"

"Do you know what you're getting yourself into?" He felt the pressure of her leg against his thigh as it looped over his.

Jessie tilted her head back and looked up into his face. "Sometimes, Ridgefield," she said, "you ask too many questions."

"Is that so?"

"Yep. And here you thought *I* was the one." Her fingers traveled across his chest, then up to the side of his face. The rough beard tickled her fingers.

"Jessie, are you sure?"

Jessie's fingers threaded into his hair. "Matt, there are few certainties in life. But some things seem right, you know?"

There was more than pressure on his thigh bothering Matt now. He'd wanted Jessie for so long. When he breathed in, it was the smell of her that filled him. When she brushed her lips on his neck, he thought he was going to explode. "Yeah," he managed, "I know."

"And this seems right."

The last words were lost as Matt pushed forward on the couch until he was standing. Without any more talk, he lifted Jessie's white-robed body in his arms and carried her up the winding steps.

Seven

Jessie nuzzled her head into the hollow of Matt's shoulder and wound her arms around his neck. She felt weightless, secure and in a world entirely different from the one in which she usually lived. She had a sense of rightness, of everything in her life congealing into this one moment and fitting perfectly: her past, the present and her future.

There was a small light on in the bedroom, which Matt had turned on when Jessie had bathed. It cast warm shadows across the thick down comforter that covered Matt's wide bed. It felt like a puffy cloud when he lowered her body on to it.

Jessie lay there, her head on the pile of pillows, his fleecy robe wrapped around her, and she looked up at Matt.

He stood quietly, his heart expanding each second, his eyes filled with desire.

Jessie's breath caught in her throat. The love she felt was staggering. It was an enormous feeling, cutting off everything else. She lifted her hand and tugged him until he sat down on the bed beside her.

"Jessie," Matt started. His voice was deep and husky. The single word caught in his throat and he began again. "Jessie, I've wanted to love you for so long."

Still lying on the pillows, Jessie didn't answer. Instead she began to undo the buttons on his shirt while he watched. She was innocence and vamp all wrapped up in one, a lovely sensuous creature who was making him feel things with an intensity he'd never experienced before. For a second he wondered about those feelings, but as Jessie's fingers began to play on the skin beneath his shirt, clear thought was lost. "You're bewitching me, Jessie." He pulled his arms out of his shirt.

"Maybe I am," she whispered. "All I know is that I want to be with you." She shook her head. "No, I'll say it. I want to love you."

Emotions moved across her face, and Matt felt a tenderness swell up inside him that mixed with desire and shot through his body. He threaded his fingers through her hair and leaned down to kiss her.

"Wait." Jessie pressed her palms flat against his chest. Matt frowned.

"I want to look at you for a minute. You're beautiful, you know."

Matt's laughter came from deep in his throat.

"I mean it, Matt."

Matt reached down and undid the belt of her robe.

"From that first day," she was saying, her words slowing down as he pushed the edges of the robe back, "I thought you were..."

Matt slipped the robe off her shoulders and her arms fell out readily, and then she lay naked, the soft robe a bed beneath her. "What were you saying about beauty?" he breathed, his heartbeat racing and his mind filled with the image of her. Her breasts were firm and full and heated with a flush that spread up to the hollow of her throat. Her skin glistened in the muted light. He dipped his head and kissed her breasts until he felt the nipples grow firm and pointed beneath his lips and tongue. Jessie made small noises that fed his desire and he held back, stopping for a moment to slow down. Jessie was a gift that had somehow ended up here with him. The reasons for it eluded him. But here she was, the woman he had spent weeks mentally putting out of his bed. Here she was in all her beauty and for the first time in longer than he could remember, Matt Ridgefield wanted to bring complete pleasure to someone else. He sat upright and smiled down at her.

"Are you going somewhere?" Jessie asked across the shadowy space. She wore a small smile and her eyes were deep with desire.

"Not on your life." Matt stood then and pulled off his clothes in a few rough tugs.

He stood there for a minute above her, naked and powerful. Jessie stared at his body, at the lean lines of his hips, the broad, muscled torso and the thatch of brown curling hair on his chest. She wanted to touch him, to feel each part of him. Their eyes locked and for a moment it seemed to Jessie that their shared desire was on fire, a force mightier than both of them and blinding in its power. Her body responded and she moved on the bed, unable to still herself. "I think I need you down here now," she said in a choked voice.

"And I think you're the most wonderful thing to happen to me in a long, long time, Jessie." He slid down on the bed next to her, propping himself up on one elbow. His finger traced an intricate design across her breasts.

No one had ever spoken her name quite like that before, Jessie thought. Jessie had never sounded sensuous and beautiful. It had always been the name of an ordinary woman who went about her simple life, but suddenly it spoke of someone else, someone exotic and desirable. "I think this was meant to be, Matt."

"My beautiful fatalist." Skillfully he fondled the warm fullness of her breasts.

Jessie moaned. "You're asking for trouble, bub."

"That's an interesting way to look at it." Matt cupped her breast in one hand and leaned down to brush it with a kiss. Restraint was becoming difficult again. She was so desirable, so beautiful that his senses were on overload. This was far more than a tryst, and the knowledge of that only fueled his desire. He felt himself growing hard against her side.

Jessie responded with a dreamy smile. She reached up and pressed her palm against his face. The rough stubble of his beard tickled her hand. "Hmm, this is sexy."

"Grown for the occasion," he murmured, his fingers moving down to caress the smooth plane of her abdomen.

"It's not the only thing that's grown."

"Jessie, you surprise me," Matt said, grinning down at her. His fingers were traveling lovingly across her smooth, warm flesh, dipping lower until they stopped by the curling nest of hair. He cupped it in the palm of his hand and pressed gently.

Jessie moaned. Her breathing came in starts and stops. "Do you have any idea what you're doing to me?"

"I hope so," Matt said and then he stopped further talk with his lips, kissing her with a growing hunger while his fingers, gentle but demanding, sought entrance below.

Jessie twisted frantically, her back arched, and she gasped. The weight of her desire was suffocating. She was burning up inside. Everything in her screamed for Matt. Without him she would die. "I want you so much. Now, Matt, now."

Matt plunged inside her, forcing himself, with enormous strength of mind and will, to be gentle, to go slowly, to bring Jessie with him to the perfect summit of ecstasy. She deserved that and so much more. "You're part of me now, my love," he murmured into her hair, his body throbbing with the pleasure of her.

"There's nowhere else for me to be." She amazed herself that an earthly voice could still come from a body that had left earth. She was soaring in space, buoyed by a love so intense it would have frightened her had any of those merely mortal feelings been left. But they hadn't, so all she felt was delicious, excruciating, delirious joy.

And afterward, when she and Matt slowly descended back to earth, swaying and floating like two beautiful, entwined autumn leaves, the joy collected into a lovely, tender treasure inside her heart. She curled up next to Matt, his body curved so that she fit snugly into his side, and slept.

Matt watched her sleep. Every now and then he reached out and ran his hand along her cheek or pushed away a curl from her eyelid, or brushed a finger against the warm rise of her breast.

Jessie had done something to him. He wasn't sure just yet what it was, but he was a different person from the man who had followed her into a bagel store. The change had been gradual, he supposed, but loving her tonight had brought everything into bold relief and he knew it was far more than the joy of their bodies together. Somehow, somewhere along the line between the bagel store and here, Jessie Sager had sneaked inside of him and taken up residence. And he, Matt Ridgefield, was more of a person because of it.

What he was feeling for her went far beyond anything he'd ever felt before, but he wasn't willing to name it. He hadn't neglected his physical needs over the years; there'd been women who wanted the same thing he did—physical satisfaction, some companionship, no ties. Matt had been careful to step aside if unwanted emotions crept in, and he'd always been discreet in choosing his lovers. But Jessie was in another category. He sure as hell hadn't gone after this, whatever it was that was making him feel more complete than he had in a lifetime. Maybe all Jessie's talk of preordained stuff wasn't merely frivolous.

Matt stroked her hair and thought of astronauts and pilots who had dared to break incredible barriers. That's what Jessie had done, broken through a barrier. And she probably hadn't even been trying. Did the men in space, soaring beyond the laws we'd lived with for so many years, feel as he did?

Jessie shifted slightly in her sleep, and Matt moved to accommodate her position. No one had ever felt this way, Matt was sure of it.

And with the knowledge that he was, in fact, the bearer of an incredible gift, he fell to sleep.

Hours later, when the early light of dawn began to lighten the room, Jessie stirred. A lovely soft blanket of warmth covered her. She opened one eye and angled her head to the right. Matt's bare chest filled her small area of vision. She watched curiously as his chest lifted and lowered in a slow rhythmic pattern of breathing. It was a powerful, wonderful chest and she tugged at the comforter, pulling it up to Matt's neck to bury her more completely with him. She moved her legs gently and they brushed against, then overlapped his. Limbs entwined beneath a body-warmed tent. His nakedness against hers was delicious. It was better than breakfast in bed, she thought, this waking up with Matt beside her. Better than hot coffee and bagels and even Bagels, Bialys and Blintzes' weekend special—bagels, lox and cream cheese. Her silly ruminations brought a smile to her lips and she pressed the smile against the solid flesh of his upper arm. She hadn't kissed him there before; it tasted wonderful. Where else hadn't she kissed him? she wondered, and her body squirmed helplessly beneath the thought.

Beneath the covers her arm crept over his stomach, pulling him closer to her. She moved her hand upward and with her palm flat, she lightly rubbed his chest, stopping when her fingers touched the small firm nipples. A movement beneath the covers stopped her, and she felt a warm pressure against her thigh. Her eyes lifted to Matt's face.

One eye opened slowly. "You did it," he said huskily.

She put her fingers against his lips. Her touch was light. "This is something crazy, Ridgefield. I know about out-of-body experiences but what do you call this?"

"Very much 'in-body.'"

"Shh. I mean I can't control it. I want to love you for seventy-six hours straight. I want to feel every single inch of you pressed against me. I can't bear the thought of air coming between us. What do you think?"

Matt traced an imaginary line around the plump rise of one breast. "Sounds good to me."

"Matt, listen to me."

"You have a freckle on this breast, did you know that?" He kissed the small spot.

"No one...ever mentioned it before," she said, her breath coming in short spurts.

"Let's see what else we can find." His fingers explored her naked flesh with infinite, tender caresses until Jessie moaned uncontrollably, and Matt, beneath the comforter's hidden warmth, quickly made words superfluous. All that mattered was each new joy they were finding in each other.

The next morning, Jessie and Matt explored the small town of Evergreen with their bodies pressed together as close as small-town decorum permitted. Jessie loved the feel of her fingers in his large grip. And she loved the town. It was exactly the kind of place she'd like to live in. Not alone, of course, but if she ever married and had children. It was close enough to Manchester to have city fun, but far enough away to be away.

Matt led her into a hardware store. Jessie watched as the sixtyish-looking man behind the wooden counter greeted Matt by name. She was surprised, then scolded herself for being so stupid. He'd lived here for years now. If *someone* didn't know him, it would be terribly strange. And yet she realized in that moment that she was unused to thinking about Matt with connections because he had made it clear there were very few in his life, and that was by choice.

"Nice day to have guests, Mr. Ridgefield," the older man said.

"It sure is." Matt spoke to the hardware store owner but all the while he looked at Jessie.

"First time I remember you havin' guests," the man added.

"I guess it is, Mr. Carey."

"Well, it's mighty nice, and it's nice to meet you, miss." Jessie smiled.

"You come again now, you hear? Gets mighty lonesome and cold up here in the wintertime. Folks need guests."

Jessie wasn't sure what Matt's answer was or if he answered at all, but the lovely feel of him next to her made it immaterial. She'd tuck aside the thought of warming Matt's winter and play with it later.

After Matt had purchased some copper tubing to fix an electrical problem in his basement, they left the store. He pointed out the town square, the park where band concerts were held in nice weather, the school and a huge modern supermarket that looked out of place next to the apothecary.

Matt shrugged. "Well," he said, "you can't stop all progress. People need Pampers and Cocoa Bran even out here."

Jessie laughed, tilting her head back to look up into his face. "I love it here, Matt. I don't ever want to leave."

Now Matt laughed, intrigued by her comments, her outlook on life, the way she moved her head when she talked. Even the tiny mole on her earlobe fascinated him. And if she rubbed against him once more he'd probably have to sweep her up and carry her off to the alley behind old man Carey's hardware store.

"Mr. Ridgefield, hello!"

Jessie and Matt both looked up into the cheerful eyes of a woman about thirty years old. A brown-haired youngster with a sweep of freckles across his nose was clutching her hand tightly and she carried a curly-haired baby girl on one hip.

"Hello, Helen," Matt said.

The woman looked from Matt to Jessie, then back to Matt again. Her face was filled with apology. "Mr. Ridgefield, I'm terribly sorry. I didn't know you had guests. I would have—" She stopped, uncertain what to say next, then simply smiled and held her hand out to Jessie. "Hello. I live down the road from Mr. Ridgefield, and had I known there was someone else there, I would have planned the meals better.''

''So you're Helen,'' Jessie said. She smiled at the woman who wasn't much older than herself. ''Matt has said such nice things about you—''

Matt broke in then and completed the introductions. ''Because of Helen and her husband John,'' he said, ''my place survives in spite of me.''

''Well, I know from firsthand experience you're a terrific cook, Helen.'' She looked down at the little boy who was staring at her with beautiful wide blue eyes that matched his mother's. ''And I know you have beautiful children,'' she added.

''I'm Danny,'' the little boy announced, deciding to trust her. ''That's Sheila. She don't talk.''

Jessie admired the baby while Matt and Helen discussed the broken fence and Danny kicked pebbles into the street, explaining to Jessie that he could kick farther than his dad.

Helen assured Matt that John would take care of the fence during the week.

''In that case, let me run back to Carey's and pick up some nails. Excuse me, ladies.'' He nodded, then disappeared, leaving the two women alone.

They stood quietly for a moment, watching Danny poke a gnarled stick through a sewer grate. Then Jessie said, ''You keep Matt's house looking terrific.'' It was an inane comment, she knew, an obvious attempt to fill the void, but Helen smiled graciously.

''Oh, it's nothing. Not considering what Mr. Ridgefield has done for John and me.'' Her eyes warmed when she talked about Matt. ''He pays us twice as much as appropriate for taking care of the place. And that's in addition to what he's done for the kids.'' She pulled Danny away from the curb with one hand and smiled back at Jessie. "He's a wonder, and we think a great deal of him."

"He's helped your children?"

"Well, helped isn't the right word. Both of ours have college funds; they'll be able to go anywhere they want because of him. And Sheila was born in the new wing of the hospital that was built with Ridgefield money though no one's supposed to know it." She looked around, then brushed a loose hair from her face and went on. "Since you're his friend, there's no harm in telling you, I don't think. Maybe you know it already. Mr. Ridgefield is a hard man to figure out. He's quiet and aloof from most of the folks in Evergreen, but he has helped the town survive. It's not easy, you know, being so small."

Jessie listened, nodding, unsure how to respond. She hadn't expected to discover a new dimension to Matt so soon after getting to know the last one so intimately. It was almost an intrusion, an input of information she wasn't ready to process yet. She didn't want to touch the Matt she was so tightly wrapped in—Matt as incredible lover and friend—with any other persona. But she would have to, of course.

Matt had told her about his inheritance, and the clipping she'd found had made reference to it as well. But it hadn't really registered. It hadn't been important, maybe that was why. But seeing how Matt had used some of his considerable wealth *was* important, and the significance of it rested inside her like a special gift. There was much to learn about this man she was busy loving.

Busy loving. The thought brought an enormous smile to her face that Helen noticed, misinterpreted and made her say, "I know, I know, he's truly a generous man. And I can't tell you how glad I am to see he's brought someone out here. We worry about him being alone so much."

Only the end of Helen's sentence registered with Jessie. She wanted to assure Helen she'd do her level best to keep Matt from being lonely but she had no idea how the words would come out. Unwilling to stretch Matt's fine reputation, she kept quiet.

Helen shifted the baby from one hip to the other. Her clear eyes looked at Jessie directly. "It isn't any of my business, Jessie, but I can see you like Mr. Ridgefield a lot, and even though my opinion doesn't matter, I'm glad."

"Well, I'm—" A glimpse of Matt walking through the door of the hardware store snatched Jessie's thoughts away. It also snatched away her breath. And she suspected her poise had gone right down the sewer with the stone little Danny was carefully dropping through the grates. Could Helen see the love spread across her face like a *New York Times* headline? She raised one hand to her face as if covering the blush that would turn her into a respectable citizen again.

"Hi," Matt said. "Everything's taken care of." He settled his hand at the back of Jessie's neck, his fingers curving around it playfully. "Guess we'd better be moving on. Nice seeing you, Helen."

He and Jessie stood and watched Helen and her kids walk down the street toward a Ford pickup parked in front of the supermarket. As soon as they were out of earshot, Matt leaned over and whispered in Jessie's ear. "Three hours left—and counting—before we have to return to Manchester. What do you think?"

Think? How could she think with his warm breath tickling the skin on her cheek. "Three hours?" she managed to croak.

"How about fifteen minutes for an ice cream at Daisy's? It's homemade and there isn't any better. Then we might want to head back."

"We might want to do that," Jessie agreed, her heart swelling.

They finished double scoops of white-chocolate mousse on the way back to the car. Jessie licked a trickle of sweet cream from her finger. "You're right." She sighed. "It's heaven. What more could a girl want?"

Matt took the question to heart, and when he and Jessie pulled into the gates of the farm a short while later, he had two and a half hours left to show her.

Eight

The next two weeks went by in a whirl. Stopping to think rationally was a luxury Jessie refused to allow herself, except when it came to work. She dealt with Matt on a totally different plane. Her love lifted her up to it, and she felt sustained and safe there. She was happy for the moment simply to bask in the sheer joy of loving Matt. Surely everyone was allowed one moment like this in a lifetime, she told herself, a time to be joyous and free and deliriously happy. Yes, surely this was her due. She would consider the future in the future.

Her incredible energy transferred to everything. She managed to rise earlier, visit with Emma each day before she went to the office, and her work at Bourke and Bailey was going great guns. The manuscript on Alexander Ridgefield began to pile up on her old oak desk.

"Do you have elves who come in at night?" Marilyn asked one morning. She eyed the impressive stack of computer printouts.

Jessie laughed. "Actually, it's the fellow himself. Alexander and I have become fast friends. He tells me what to say and I just write it down. Every writer should have it so easy."

Marilyn nodded, half listening. "I saw Matt this morning. We had breakfast together."

"Good. He doesn't always eat breakfast. It's the most important meal of the day."

"He was more talkative than I've seen him in some time."

Jessie looked up from her work. She wished she could smile normally when she thought about Matt. It was a dead giveaway, that silly, kind of lopsided look that slid across her face. But she seemed helpless to control it. "Oh?" she managed to say.

"He seems very happy, Jessie," the older woman told her quietly.

Jessie's smile faded. "Marilyn, does that bother you?"

"No, not how you're thinking. I don't play games with people, Jessie, and Matt and I have no ties like that. Ours are the kind I have with you now, those of very good friends."

"Do I hear a *but* at the end of that?"

"No 'buts,' not really." Marilyn walked over and poured herself a cup of coffee from a pot Jessie kept near her computer. "I love you both. If you're making each other happy, that's great. I'm thrilled for you."

Jessie's eyes didn't leave Marilyn's face. "But you're worried, aren't you?"

"Not worried exactly..."

"You don't want to see our grand citadel of love and romance crumble with us lying beneath it, crushed to smithereens."

Marilyn laughed. "Jessie, you should try writing."

Jessie stood up and gave Marilyn a hug. "You *are* a good friend, Marilyn. The best. But I don't think you have to worry. Matt and I have been totally up-front with each other. There are no hidden surprises."

Jessie knew exactly why Marilyn was worried. About a week ago, the two women had had dinner together on the night that Matt had attended a faculty dinner. They had talked until two in the morning. Through laughter and tears they had erased the age barrier forever as they shared the grit and the grist of their past lives.

Jessie had learned that Marilyn's parents had tried to help Matt after his parents' deaths. Marilyn took her back in time to what Matt was like as a teenager, to how he had idolized his father and dearly loved his mother. The perfect family, their friends and acquaintances had thought. She shared with Jessie the agony of that day and the years after. She explained how Matt had changed, become withdrawn, then finally had tentatively picked up old relationships again. But they were irrevocably changed. No one got too close to Matt, and the women he dated all knew that commitment was no part of him. He would never chance the responsibility of someone else's life or of ruining it the way his father had almost done to his.

It was an awful irony, Marilyn told Jessie, but she thought that if Matt had loved his father less, had thought less of him, he might not have been destroyed. But he had seen his hero crumble. If it could happen to Matt's father, it could happen to anyone.

Jessie had listened intently because anything about Matt was important to her. But the intensity of her love was far too strong for her to hear messages or warnings in any of what Marilyn shared. Her mind couldn't handle the future yet because it was so filled with the overwhelming present.

Now Marilyn stood in Jessie's office in a stripe of yellow sunshine slanting across the floor. She listened, watched the beautiful glow on Jessie's face and then smiled. "Okay. It's great to see two people so happy. I'll stop worrying and leave well enough alone."

"No, you won't. But that's only one of the reasons we love you. Now tell me, which of these pictures of the mayor should we use in the final chapter?"

Marilyn concentrated on the two photos Jessie held up, and shoved the worry to the back of her mind. She picked out one of the pictures and the rest of the morning was spent discussing publishing details and making color decisions for the cover of *The Manchester Rogue*. It was a far easier task to handle for both of them than considering what kind of future could exist for Jessie and Matt.

Matt sat in his office, his hands clasped behind his head, and told Dena she should order more flowers.

"The same kind as yesterday, Professor Ridgefield?" Dena asked.

Matt pondered her question with the gravity due a faculty review meeting. "Nope," he said finally. "I don't want her place to start looking like a funeral parlor, but it definitely needs cheering up. How about one of those trees people grow in their houses? Could we send one of them?"

"We can sure try, Professor," Dena said. Being a part of this wonderful romance had Dena beside herself. And being the bearer of the juiciest gossip to hit the staff lounge in a long time was also kind of nice. She headed for the phone to see if McMann's florist delivered trees.

* * *

"Matt, a tree?" Jessie stood in the middle of her tiny apartment early that evening, her eyes wide with incredulity. The ficus tree was huge and, to fit it in, Jessie had had to push the kitchen table flat against one wall.

Matt watched her face light up. "This place needed something alive."

"I'd say I'm pretty alive," Jessie said, snuggling up to him.

Matt's arm wrapped around her instinctively. "No argument there." He nuzzled the soft skin at her neck. "Mmm, you smell terrific. What is it?"

Jessie's throaty laugh circled about him and did its magic on parts of him he'd given up trying to control.

"It's chicken," she said. "*Moo goo gai pan.* I decided to cook for you tonight."

Matt glanced over her shoulder at several white take-out cartons lined up along the counter. "Great," he said. Then he turned her around until she faced him fully. Her breasts pressed into his chest and the top of her head brushed his chin. "But I know it's all a ruse to get me up here."

Jessie's head lifted back. "Drats, I blew it. The ruse is up. Now you know I meant to ply you with my charms and turn you to putty."

Matt tugged her blouse from beneath the waist band of her jeans and slipped his hands across her back. "But I'm made of steel, woman. No one seduces me."

Lifting up on the toes of her tennis shoes, she found his lips. "I know," she murmured, her breath warm on his face. "O mighty man of iron—"

"Steel," Matt corrected. He shifted slightly and then slid one hand around to her stomach, then up the smooth skin to capture one breast. He kneaded it gently.

"Steel, oh, yeah," she said, her breath coming in starts and stops. "Like my heart. That's what you've done, you know. How...how did you do that?" Her eyes were glazed when her head fell back.

"I dunno," Matt said huskily. "But let's see if that's true." He unbuttoned her blouse then and pulled it apart. Jessie's breath caught in her throat. Matt dipped his head and pressed his lips against the side of her breast, then moved around until his lips circled it slowly with infinite gentleness. His tongue flicked with small, sure movements. "Is that where your heart's supposed to be?" His words rose up to her, a slow and seductive cadence.

Jessie moaned. "Matt, the dinner—"

"Will wait, m'love. I promise. Finding your heart's far more important." In one smooth movement, Matt lifted her from the thin braided rug and carried her off to the tiny alcove that was filled with Jessie's bed.

On Wednesday, Jessie arrived at the office and couldn't work. It had been two days since she had seen Matt.

She had spent Monday evening with Emma, taking her out for pizza and buying new barrettes for her hair. Emma was feeling good and looking better than she had for a few weeks. Jessie wondered if her joy was catching, and for a brief moment she imagined the wonder of being able to share enough of what she felt with Emma, so that Emma would be cured.

The next night she had a meeting and Matt had called her late. He had gone out to the farm for the night to check on some things, and he and Jessie stayed on the phone until nearly dawn. Jessie, in her warm-ups, imagined herself out there with him, warming the four-poster.

But his voice wasn't enough. She needed to see him. Right now. Is that what addicts felt like? Jessie wondered as she stood and leafed through the manuscript pages on the desk. The need to see Matt was almost a painful one, a craving inside of her that needed to be satisfied. She put the papers down and looked at them intently. "How about a coffee break, Alexander?" Hearing no disagreement, she patted the manuscript affectionately and hurried out of the building.

When she showed up at Matt's classroom, the door was ajar, left open by some late student, she supposed. But it suited her purpose fine. She could slip right in without chancing a squeaky hinge. The door was in the back and Jessie quickly sat down in the last row. The room was a small amphitheater with the rows elevated and the teacher down in front. Matt was walking back and forth, his hands moving in the air, and talking. His voice reached up to her seconds after she sat down. It was deep and rich and pulled her into his lecture. He was talking about the Age of Enlightenment to the room full of gangly students.

Jessie listened carefully, not caring as much about the words as the look on Matt's face and the inflections of his voice, which made the students nod or shake their heads. She rested her chin in the palms of her hands and watched as he pressed and prodded the students into thinking, as he rubbed his strong chin already shadowed with beard, as he looked off into the distance, pulling the right words out of nowhere to explain his point. His arms and hands helped him teach. He would reach out in an intimate gesture or lift his broad palms upward, offering them an idea to latch on to. His voice was seductive even here, and she knew he wasn't at all aware of it. It was his teaching voice and with it he was luring young minds into a new world. Jessie felt her heart stretch.

When Matt dismissed the class a short while later, Jessie couldn't move. She was glued to the chair, mesmerized. Matt took the steps in four long strides and was at her side.

"I don't believe I signed your audit slip, miss."

Jessie looked up. "Then I guess you better do that." She held her head back. "But I don't have a pencil."

"Any professor worth his salt knows how to improvise."

"I thought as much."

Matt leaned over, bracing himself with his hands. His head was inches away from hers. "You inspired me, sitting back here."

"Then I get the audit permission?" Jessie asked, her eyes bright.

"You got it," he said, and sealed it with his lips, hungrily tasting the delight that had been denied him for two days.

It might have gone on indefinitely, but a slight noise in the distance entered the outer corners of Jessie's consciousness. She pulled away, just far enough to speak. "Matt," she murmured softly, "I think we have company."

The sound took shape then, and Matt turned around to the delighted applause of a dozen students who had come in for a class on early twentieth-century thought and instead had been treated to a page out of *Gone With The Wind*.

Matt and Jessie separated reluctantly. For all his good breeding and upper-crust decorum, Matt was sorely tempted to ignore the interruption and get back to things that mattered. Jessie. But he didn't. With regret he headed down to the podium. And when Jessie called after him that she couldn't see him for dinner because she was taking Emma out for a hamburger, Matt surprised and pleased her by uncharacteristically inviting himself along.

* * *

"I didn't think you liked kids much," she said to him on the ride over to the orphanage.

"I never said I didn't like kids. I said I didn't want to father them."

"Oh."

"Besides, this is the only way I get to see you tonight."

Jessie looked out the window. Vague unrest had come from somewhere and was settling in the pit of her stomach. She wanted to ignore it. It was a mixture of things bothering her and she couldn't bring herself to separate them out and deal with each separately. There was Matt. There was Emma and her illness. There was Jessie in love. It was all too much to think about so she told herself she was just hungry, that was all. Her eyes settled on the brilliant red sun sinking behind the Manchester skyline. Sunsets, she decided, she could deal with.

When Emma bounced out to the car looking anything but sick, Jessie's heart lifted and the gloom was blown away by the young girl's brilliant smile.

"You remember Matt?" Jessie asked when Emma was settled between them in the front seat.

Emma nodded. She looked up at him, her thick brown lashes shadowing her cheeks. "Are you going with us?"

"Only if it's okay with you," Matt said.

Emma thought about it for a minute, her fingers absently rubbing the smooth leather of the car seat. Matt had shown up, not in the Jeep or his Beetle, but in an ice-blue Saab that smelled of creamy leather and after-shave.

Jessie watched Emma as the girl considered the situation. Usually, when she took Emma out to eat they rode the bus, or Jessie borrowed her neighbor Amanda's old Chevy. Emma was enjoying this moment of luxury.

"Sure," Emma finally replied. "You can come."

Matt grinned. It felt a little like winning the distinguished teaching award.

Jessie saw his smile and decided not to tell him it was his car that had won Emma over.

The hamburgers at Earnest Ernie's Hamburger Heaven were the biggest and juiciest in town, and Emma adored the place. Occasionally Jessie pointed out that the burgers were also the greasiest in all of Connecticut, but it didn't deter Emma. She always ordered the same thing—a double burger with the works, large fries and a chocolate shake.

"Is that what you recommend?" Matt asked.

"Yes," Emma answered, closing the grease-spotted menu and expertly sliding it back into the rack on the wall. "Except sometimes Jessie gets the triple burger."

Matt lifted his brows and looked over at Jessie. "Oh?"

Jessie shrugged. "I need my daily dose of grease just like the next guy."

Emma giggled.

After the waitress left with their order, Emma pulled a crumpled slip of paper from her pocket and pushed it across the table to Jessie.

"Wish list?"

Emma nodded.

"Okay, good." Jessie took it and put it into her purse.

Matt watched the transaction silently. Before he had a chance to inquire about it, Emma turned the conversation to a dance she was teaching the little kids at school, and Matt filed his question away for later.

"I almost forget she's sick," he said to Jessie after they had dropped off an exhausted Emma at the home.

Jessie nodded. "Me, too, at first. But when I hugged her I could feel that her glands were swollen again. And there are other little things like the fact that she ate one bite of her hamburger and two French fries.''

"I thought maybe that was a part of the ritual."

"No, she used to eat the whole damn hamburger. Every bite. And sometimes helped me.'' When her voice cracked, Matt reached across the seat and Jessie's fingers curled readily into his palm. He held them tightly.

"It's tough," he said.

"Yeah.'' Jessie fell silent.

As they neared Jessie's apartment, Matt asked about the crumpled sheet of paper.

"I promised Emma a trip someday. She's never been out of Manchester that she remembers. So one day, the two of us are going to the big city for a weekend and we're going to do it up right.'' Jessie pulled the paper from her purse and smoothed it out on her knee. When they stopped near the street light, she held it up and read it.

"It says, 'Blueberry waffles.' '' Jessie laughed. "I told Emma to keep a list of things she'd like to do when we go. The collection is growing. We may have to stay away a year instead of a weekend to get everything in.''

"She's a sweet kid. She deserves it. When are you going?"

Jessie shrugged. "Maybe I'll be able to take her when this book is done and the last payment comes. I want it to be nice.''

Matt nodded. "Sure."

"For not liking kids—excuse me, for not liking to father kids, you get along with them just fine," Jessie said.

"Emma's a nice kid.''

"You only like nice kids?"

"What is this, Jess? Am I on trial here?''

Jessie shook her head. "Of course not. I'm tired, that's all.'' Tired, and in love with a man with whom she could have no future. The words crept in, unwanted, disliked, and she tried to force them away.

"Do you want me to come up?" Matt asked.

Jessie was quiet for a moment.

"Matt," she finally said, "I always want you to come up. I always want you with me, you've become a part of me. But I think if I don't catch up on some sleep, I'm going to be an unfit friend."

"But never an unfit lover." She had looked at Matt with such love in her eyes that, although disappointed, he couldn't take offense.

When he held her face between his palms and kissed her good-night, Jessie knew with a surge of renewed faith that it would be okay, that the rough feelings disturbing her joy would pass. They had to.

Without planning to, Jessie now spent nearly every weekend at the farm with Matt, and her initial love for the rolling green acres only grew deeper. It amazed her, when the realization struck, that she had never, not once, felt like a guest at Applewood Farm. From the beginning it had possessed her—and she, it—in a strange, otherworldly way. She supposed it was those childhood dreams that were responsible. Every now and then she had to stop and remind herself that it was Matt's house, not hers, and that he was only sharing it with her as he would any good friend.

"Matt," she said one Saturday, "do you mind if I make some pillows for the porch chaises?"

Matt looked around. They were having coffee out on the porch, knowing it would be one of the last times until next spring they would have that option. Even today the wind was crisp and both Jessie and Matt wore heavy sweaters.

"If you have the time," he replied, "that would be great. If not we can buy some at one of the craft shops in town."

"I'd rather make them. Then some of me will be here all the time."

"It already is," Matt told her without even bothering to temper his words. He usually paused before he spoke, unwilling to mention anything that would promise things to Jessie he couldn't live up to. He thought all the time about protecting her, about not hurting her, about being honest and open with her. What he refused to think about was how he was falling in love with her.

Jessie looked over at him and smiled. "That was a nice thing to say."

"It's the truth." He was speaking slowly now, carefully. "I thought this place was perfect. It filled all my needs, I could drive out here and be completely myself. I didn't want other people here. And then you came." Matt put down his coffee cup and looked out through the screens. He leaned forward, pushing his forearms onto his knees, and stared straight ahead, his brows drawn together. His eyes focused on the trees, searching for something out there, as if answers were tangled up in the gnarled branches of the sturdy Connecticut maples that stood outside the porch door. He shook his head, then looked over at Jessie. "You've changed things, Jess. When I come out here alone now, I feel an absence."

Jessie wrapped her arms around herself. No, that didn't do the trick. She rose from the chair, crossed the porch and snuggled down next to Matt, pulling his arms tight about her. There. That was much better.

Nine

Jessie knew she should have talked to Matt first. But there hadn't been time. No, that wasn't really true. Who was she kidding? There had been time. She'd been with him every possible moment for weeks now. He'd even gone along with her a couple of times when she'd visited Emma. The plain truth was that a part of Matt still escaped her understanding, and she hadn't the foggiest idea what he would say to this. Marilyn had thought it was a wonderful idea. She had even volunteered to help. But then Marilyn wasn't Matt. Nor was Applewood Farm hers. Well, Matt had a perfect right to say no, that was sure. It was his place, after all.

Jessie stuffed her hands into her pockets and slowed her jog to a fast walk. Usually exercise helped calm her down and brought sensible perspective back into her life. Today it made her insides feel as if they'd been in the blender.

She rounded the corner and sprinted the rest of the way back to her apartment. She was being silly. Matt was a kind, generous human being and even though he didn't want to father kids, he must like them. He liked Emma, Jessie could see that now, even after he'd tried to tell her the reason he hung around them was to be with her. He even had a nice way with the little girl, which had surprised Jessie. His manner was easy, not forced, and Emma responded to him nicely. No, Matt wasn't going to mind this at all.

She and Matt were going to dinner at Marilyn's and Jessie would explain it all to him at some propitious moment during the evening. She'd tell him how one of the nuns had mentioned how lovely it would be if they could get the children out to the country just once before bad weather set in. The outing, Sister Maria had said, would be therapeutic. Like squirrels storing things away before the onslaught of winter, the children could store away a little sunshine and fresh air to help them through those dreary months. But where would they go that wouldn't be too rustic and would have the amenities the children needed? Jessie knew just the place.

"Matt, you're early!" Jessie stopped short at the bottom step leading up to her apartment building. Matt was standing at the top dressed in an elegant, gray suede sports jacket.

When they came together these days, Matt never heard Jessie's first words. He was too taken by her, and until he had wrapped her in his arms and kissed her, he couldn't concentrate on mundane things like conversation. He was down the steps in three easy strides.

"Hmm," he murmured into her damp hair. "That's sexy."

"My sweat?" Jessie said, pulling slightly away to inhale. Her heart pounded wildly, a reaction that was now as expected as the sunrise.

"The sensual tang of exercise. It's an ancient aphrodisiac, Jess."

"You're making that up," Jessie said, looping her arm around his waist and tugging him along beside her as they went inside. Together they walked up the two flights of stairs to her apartment.

Once inside, Matt leaned against the closed door. "Jessie, you have to move out of this place."

Jessie poured herself a glass of water, then turned around and leaned against the sink, her laughing eyes focused on Matt. "You may not know it, Matt, but you have the greatest looking calves in Manchester, and it's all because of my steps. Be thankful."

"Okay." Matt came toward her and trapped her against the sink, one arm on either side of her, "Let me thank you properly."

"For your healthy calves?"

"Uh-huh." He kissed her masterfully, his lips coming down on hers in slow, familiar possession.

When he finally pulled away, Jessie's breathing was labored and she felt a new sheen of perspiration covering her forehead and throat and sliding down between her breasts. "You are one hell of a kisser, Professor Ridgefield," she said.

"Thank you. Want to see what else I can do?" His hands slipped beneath her T-shirt and flattened out on her back. With his fingers, Matt made gentle rotating movements on her skin.

Jessie moaned at the delicious sensations that floated through her body.

"I can do other things, too," Matt whispered into her ear.

"I know," Jessie gasped. "But will Marilyn understand if I show up for dinner unintelligible, in a wet T-shirt, my eyes glazed and unseeing?"

"Dunno. Want to find out?" His hands moved down and dipped beneath the elastic band of her sweatpants. He cupped her buttocks in his large palms.

"Matt." She pulled away with difficulty. She wanted more, but someone had to be in charge here and she had serious doubts that Matt would take the honors.

Matt smiled a half grin that melted her insides.

"You were easier to handle when you were a curmudgeon," Jessie said.

"Was that what I was?"

She nodded, slipping out of the cocoon he'd built for her between his body and the sink.

Matt pondered the thought while Jessie headed for her bedroom. "A curmudgeon," he mused aloud.

"You think about that while I shower. And then we can go to Marilyn's intact and respectable."

"Respectable is a relative term," Matt said. The glint in his eyes told Jessie his thoughts had strayed from "curmudgeon" and "respectable" to something far more dangerous. She hurried into the bedroom and closed the door behind her. "I'll be ready in five seconds," she announced in muffled tones through the door.

Matt headed for the couch. He sat down and settled his long legs out in front of him, his thoughts playing with the woman who was now singing faintly in the background as she showered.

Jessie had set something on fire inside him that made it difficult to sit for long periods of time. He marveled at it sometimes, at the feelings, at the pure joy she'd released in him. It was almost as if a chemical reaction had taken over all the workings of his body. When he tried to analyze it, it fuzzed and unraveled, so he settled for quiet musings that simply brought Jessie close to him when she was across town or campus, or in another room. He knew he loved Jessie. He had known that since the incredible night at the farm. Maybe he had known it even sooner, but that was the night when she had taken over his soul. His love for her was enormous, a kind of invisible atmosphere that surrounded, not only him, but his life, all happenings relevant to him. He knew he was different for it, but he didn't know what this meant in terms of his future life, or, more importantly, what it meant for Jessie.

"Ready?" Jessie appeared in the doorway, her dark hair still slightly damp. She wore little makeup—just a stroke of pink across her lips and a touch of color on her eyelids—and her clothes were plain—a forest green dress, softly gathered and curving gently over her body. And in all this simplicity there was a beauty that took Matt's breath away.

He nodded and opened the door, knowing that the slightest pause would arouse him in a way that wouldn't serve well on their arrival at Marilyn's elegant home.

"Well, Jessie," said Frederick Bourke, the distinguished gray-haired publisher who reminded Jessie of Spencer Tracy, "I need to tell you that I am enormously pleased with your work on *The Manchester Rogue*." He settled back in the upholstered dining-room chair and sipped his coffee slowly. "It's going to fit into our list very well. Very well indeed."

Marilyn leaned forward at the table. "Of course it is, Frederick. Did you have any doubts?"

"None my dear, of course not."

Feeling slightly detached, Jessie watched the interplay. The guests were all people she liked—misters Bailey and Bourke and their gracious wives, and Adam Peters, old friend and sometimes-date of Marilyn's who was a judge and who charmed Jessie with his surprising wit—but they all knew each other as Jessie did not. It was actually a nice arrangement after a busy day; she was comfortable not saying a lot, and she found eavesdropping on their world pleasant and nonthreatening.

The meal had been wonderful—delicate pieces of lobster and shrimp swimming in a spicy, buttery sauce, and a different wine, it seemed, for every morsel of food that was set on the wide linen-covered table. Jessie watched the maid masterfully handle the plates and glasses, then arrive at Marilyn's elbow with the Cherries Jubilee in an enormous silver platter. She tried to imagine Matt growing up in a household like this, surrounded by elegant, extravagant furnishings and impeccable service. He was certainly as comfortable as anyone there, and yet the thought of Matt as a youngster living in this grand, formal way made her uncomfortable.

Applewood Farm was a different story. Matt fit there perfectly. It was a natural fit, one that didn't come from breeding and education. And even though Jessie had come to appreciate the considerable wealth invested in the farm, it was different somehow. Matt's place didn't ask to be seen, it simply *was*, quiet and homey and beautiful. That it was worth a fortune was almost irrelevant.

"Matt can give you information on that, Dorothy," Marilyn was saying from the head of the table. "He owns some land in the country."

Dorothy Bourke looked over at her husband. "There, you see, Frederick? Talk to Matt before you do anything foolish."

"Is that so?" Frederick lifted his thick white brows and looked down the table at Matt. "I've been thinking of buying a place away from town, somewhere to take the grandchildren, you know. Where is your place, Matthew?"

Matt briefly explained the general direction of Applewood Farm and Jessie noticed the reluctance behind his words. It was as if he were revealing a carefully guarded family recipe.

"*If* it truly exists," Marilyn commented. "None of us, except Jessie, has ever seen the place. For years I thought Matt was having a secret affair and used this 'country place' as a cover."

Matt laughed obligingly. "I'm not that clever, Marilyn."

"Well, I'm delighted that I'll finally get to see it," Marilyn said.

Matt lifted one brow and Jessie tried desperately to nudge Marilyn's leg with her toe. Instead she managed to kick Bryan Bailey in the ankle and his muffled groan forced her to abandon her original intention. Bryan looked over at her curiously. Jessie blushed and stared down at the remnants of her Cherries Jubilee. The ice cream on her plate had melted into an unrecognizable substance and Jessie envied it.

"Oh?" Matt asked, his attention still on Marilyn.

"Yes, Matt. Jessie may not have had a chance to tell you, but I have volunteered to cook hot dogs for the kiddies."

"Hot dogs?" Matt echoed.

Jessie lifted her napkin. It wouldn't do at all to shove it in Marilyn's mouth so she twisted it until her fingers hurt from the pressure.

"Kiddies?" questioned Dorothy.

"*You're* going to cook?" Adam put in.

"Of course hot dogs," said Marilyn, addressing Matt and skipping over the other comments. "You don't serve steak to little ones!"

"Marilyn, what are you talking about?" Matt asked patiently.

Jessie sat up straight in her chair. She dropped one pale hand on his jacket sleeve. "Matt, I didn't get a chance to tell you—no, to *ask* you I mean, but—"

"It's a grand idea, Matt," Marilyn cut in. "I mean those kids need to get away. And to volunteer your farm for the picnic is truly wonderful."

Everyone around the table nodded, not quite sure what Marilyn was talking about but finding her enthusiasm contagious. Only Jessie and Matt remained still. Finally Matt looked over at Jessie. "Jessie," he said slowly, "maybe you'd better explain this."

"Yes, maybe I'd better." She looked at Marilyn and in that one sorrowful glance Marilyn understood.

Her eyes begged apology. Quickly she called the maid to refill coffee cups and hoped vaguely that the young girl would spill one in someone's lap so the subject could be changed gracefully.

Jessie laughed lightly as she looked around the table at the confused faces. "It's a simple explanation. St. Bede's Orphanage wants to have an outing, you see." She concentrated on Frederick's face. It was so fatherly and brought a comfort to her as she felt the coiled tension in Matt's body next to her. "And—" she sneaked a quick look at Matt "—having the tendency to jump into things without thinking, I told Sister Maria about Matt's wonderful place. I was going to talk to him about it tonight." She turned to Matt, forcing a calm smile on her face. "So,

Matt, that's all there is. I thought Applewood might be the perfect place for the picnic.''

"You thought . . ." Matt sought calmness.

"Yes, I did. So I told Sister Maria I'd ask you if we could use it for one day.''

"And it's a wonderful idea, Matt, an ideal place, from how Jessie describes it," Marilyn said, trying to ease the tension she could see in the tight curve of Matt's lips.

"Well," began Frederick, "frankly, I think that's noble of you, Matthew. Those kids don't have much over there. A day out in the country will do them good.''

The others agreed and Dorothy, in a move that won Jessie's undying gratitude, proceeded to entertain the group with outrageous stories of Frederick's misguided experience as a summer counselor at a farm for "unfocused youth," a group culled from a New York tenement, all of whom were well schooled in the intricacies of befuddling the older generation, particularly Frederick.

Jessie scooted far back in her chair until she could look over at Matt without his knowing it. He was paying attention to Dorothy, nodding politely, even laughing at the end of the anecdotes. But he *wasn't* looking at Jessie, and when she thought about it, she realized his leg was no longer adding warmth to hers. She wanted to reach out and touch him, but the set of his jaw stopped her. She imagined it snapping at her touch, like a shark's. Then she took a deep breath and chided herself for overreacting. When the maid came around with more dessert, she said, yes, she'd love another helping of Cherries Jubilee and she drowned her apprehension in calories.

"All right, let's have it," Matt said. They were on their way home to Jessie's apartment, feeling uncomfortable. The evening at Marilyn's had ended pleasantly and Jessie could almost fool herself into thinking she hadn't made a total mess of things. But from the tone of Matt's voice, she decided that time was up.

"I told you. I offered the use of your farm for one day. *One* day, Matt. I know it was presumptuous of me—"

"*Very* presumptuous."

"But I didn't really think you'd mind. Those forty or fifty kids get few chances to enjoy that sort of thing and—"

"That's not the point, Jessie."

"You asked for an explanation, Matt. Please let me finish." She felt far calmer now that she was accounting for her action. It all made sense, after all. Anyone would have done what she had done, and any decent person with Matt's resources would volunteer the farm's use. Matt was a decent person. Therefore—

"Go on," Matt said.

"I didn't have a chance to ask you—"

"You had plenty of chances," Matt told her quietly.

"All right!" Jessie turned on the seat until she faced him. "Okay, so I did. Unconsciously I guess I was afraid you wouldn't like the idea. But rationally I couldn't figure out why. It's a *perfect* place, Matt, and there's so much room. Surely one day wouldn't hurt anything."

"Hurt isn't the point either. Nor is my generosity at issue here. What's at issue is that you had absolutely no right to invade my privacy that way. Hell, if you'd asked, I'd have paid to send them all to Disney World if they wanted to go. But Applewood is my domain, my private place, and you had absolutely no right to offer it without checking with me."

Jessie stared at him as he was talking. Anger rose up into her chest. "What is with you, Matt? You're a wonderful man—and, I'm falling in *love* with you." Blood rushed to her face. Good grief, she picked the lousiest times to declare her feelings! But she couldn't worry about that now; it wasn't the point, either. "But you lock yourself up, away from things that matter, people who matter. It doesn't make any sense to me."

"I've never lied to you or pretended. You know what I am, you know I value my privacy."

"Because you're afraid. Because your father hurt you so badly, you've locked up a whole part of yourself. You think that if you don't depend on anyone and no one depends on you, then that horrible incident will never be repeated."

"That's not really the point, either, is it?" His voice had dropped to an icy chill and Jessie shivered. "I think you've assumed a little too much here."

It wasn't until she turned away from the frozen look on his face and out the window that Jessie realized they were in front of her apartment. She took a deep breath. "I guess we have some basic differences. I need some time to think them through."

"Maybe you do," Matt said.

Jessie didn't face him again. She thought if she did she'd burst into tears, and she didn't want to give Matt that satisfaction. "This is ridiculous," she muttered to the dashboard, and before Matt could answer, she had slipped out the door and was on her way up to her drafty apartment.

Two days disappeared and along with them, slowly but surely, every trace of Jessie's anger. Matt had left her completely alone, not calling or showing up at the publishing house for coffee as was his habit recently. She missed him terribly, and although she still had trouble with his ways, one thing was clear to her: she *had* assumed too much. Applewood *was* Matt's private domain and she had no right to offer it to others. Now the problem was what to do about it. She needed to let him know how sorry she was, and most of all, she needed to have him wrap his arms around her until she could hear his heartbeat pound against her own.

The inspiration and opportunity came the next day. When Marilyn said she was leaving early to attend a dinner board meeting of the College Grant Institute, a group providing scholastic funding for needy students, Jessie decided the time had come. Matt was also on the board and would be attending the same meeting.

She borrowed her neighbor's car, stopped briefly at the grocery store, then headed for Matt's apartment. Getting inside was going to be the problem, she knew. Windhaven Place was made up of two-story condominiums, each with its own patio. Matt's was on the end of a block of five. Jessie tried his door just in case, but it was locked up tighter than Fort Knox. She walked around to the back and slipped through the thick hedge of yew bushes that hid the private patio. The French doors were locked.

Jessie looked around. A narrow awning canopied half of the patio. And the first-story window next to the awning had a foot-sized ledge. Her face lit up. Easy as pie. She frequently sneaked out of her second-floor bedroom when she was growing up and all she'd had then was a rain trough to shinny up and down. This was a cinch. She climbed up on the windowsill, then hoisted herself easily up the metal frame of the awning and stood. The upstairs window was a few feet farther. Carefully balancing on the frame, she inched across to the slightly open window.

It was the cat, she decided later, that caused the problem. Feeling her movement, it jumped out of its resting place in the awning's sagging middle and flew at her face.

Jessie screamed, then fell through the awning onto the patio floor below.

Her body landed on a heavily padded chaise. One hip slammed against the armrest. She groaned and rubbed her hip gingerly, and then she looked up. In the middle of the awning was a gaping hole. Shreds of bright blue material flapped lightly in the breeze. Jessie moaned. Some apology, she thought. First she offered his home to strangers, then she tore his awning to shreds apologizing for the first thing. She pulled herself out of the chaise and took a deep breath. Well, she'd decide what to do about the awning later. She wasn't going to give up now. With the cat gone and the practice from the first try, she was up the side of the house, across the rim of the awning and in the slightly open window in no time.

It was eleven o'clock when Matt turned the key in the front door lock. The long, tedious meeting had taken its toll and he was exhausted. Or maybe it was Jessie, he thought, who was taking the toll. He hadn't slept well since the dinner at Marilyn's. He missed Jessie. Even the anger he felt had fueled his desire for her. She was imbedded so deeply inside him he couldn't weed her out. He needed to call her, to work this all out, to apologize for his anger. It might have been excessive, he'd admitted to himself, and he needed to admit that to Jessie, too. But mostly he needed to see her.

He felt for the light switch and when his fingers finally found it, he swore again because a small slip of paper had been taped next to it and the sharp edge sliced his finger. Matt angrily jerked a handkerchief from his pocket and wrapped it around his finger. Then he stared at the paper.

"Aphrodisiac," it read. "Any drug or agent that arouses or increases sexual desire."

Matt frowned. He had a new cleaning service, a group of spirited young women calling themselves the Sweeping Beauties. They'd flirted and joked with him the few times their paths had crossed and he supposed this was another kind of joke. Well, he was too tired to find it very funny. But when he read "Refrigerator" at the bottom, his curiosity got the best of him and he walked into the spotless kitchen and pulled open the door of his Frigidaire. On the middle shelf was a silver plate. In the center was a pile of freshly cut lemon wedges and around the outer edge, spaced evenly, was a circle of succulent, glistening oysters on half-shells. A small white note was stuck between two pieces of lemon.

Matt removed the plate from the refrigerator, wondering absently if he'd find the charge for the oysters on his cleaning bill. He read the short note.

"Oysters are an ancient, well-known aphrodisiac," it said in neat script. "Enjoy."

Matt put the plate back in the refrigerator and closed the door. It was a mildly amusing gesture, but he wondered why they thought he need aphrodisiacs. He had his own aphrodisiac—a live, lovely, beautiful one and her name was Jessie.

Matt yawned, turned out the kitchen light and went up to his bedroom. Maybe he should call Jessie tonight. No, he was exhausted. He'd call first thing in the morning, maybe take her out for bagels before work. Maybe take her somewhere more private before work.... And with that thought, he tugged off his shirt and pants, left them in a heap on the deep pile carpet, and crawled into bed.

His legs hit the lump first. Then he snaked one arm over to examine it more closely. Flesh, definitely warm and smooth. Matt's eyes shot open. He pulled back a corner of the cover.

Jessie was stark naked. "Hi," she murmured sleepily. A lock of dark hair curled over one eye.

"Jessie," Matt whispered.

"In the flesh." She giggled then, embarrassed.

"My God," he said.

"Matt—" Jessie reached out and touched his chest "—I'm so terribly sorry—"

Matt caught her fingers, lifting them up and pressing the tips to his lips. "Shh," he whispered against the soft pads. "How did you get in?"

"I broke in."

"Oh," Matt answered.

"Did you eat the oysters?"

He shook his head, his throat strangely tight.

"Want me to get them for you? There's also chilled wine at the foot of the bed. I guess you missed that."

Matt glanced across the comforter to the end of the bed. An ice bucket sat on the bench with a bottle of wine sticking out the top. "I guess I did." His hand began to wander across her belly and up between her breasts.

"I missed you, Matt," Jessie admitted into the darkness.

"'Miss' is a terribly weak word." His fingers made circles on her flesh and he could feel her soft shudders beneath his touch. "Do you know something?"

"What?" Jessie felt a sting behind her lids. There wasn't any reason, but she knew as surely as she loved Matt, that soon tears would begin to fall.

"In my whole, long life, this is the nicest surprise that I've ever had." His mouth was very close to her face and the softly spoken words misted across her cheeks.

"I've got more," Jessie said.

"I don't doubt it." Finally he kissed her, pulling her body against his own until every inch touched, hip to hip, belly to belly, breast to chest. Now the completion he felt with Jessie was beginning to return into place. He kissed her eyes, her lips and her hair.

Jessie felt herself floating, leaving the bed and the blankets and soaring higher and higher. She thought she ought to explain first, and she mumbled something about a hole in his awning, but Matt kissed away the words. And when she flinched because her hip was bruised, Matt peeled down the covers and gently kissed away everything but the most lovely sensations. Finally he lifted his head back to hers and his soft, loving words drifted around her until she couldn't hear any more, couldn't think or sort through the myriad of emotions filling her. All she could do was wrap her arms around him tightly while he entered her and filled her with unspeakable joy.

The awning would wait until morning.

Ten

Matt and Jessie didn't talk much about the St. Bede's picnic. He decided that since she had already promised his place, it should be used, and when the day was settled upon, he called his neighbors, Helen and John Berry. They agreed to help out, oversee the event and order plenty of food to feed dozens of hungry kids. When Jessie heard Matt was supplying not only the house but the food, her eyes filled with tears but Matt brushed them aside, saying he really didn't want to talk about it.

So Jessie didn't. It was awkward at first, but when she got caught up in the preparation, she completely forgot about the anger that had been a part of the process. The whole orphanage was looking forward to the outing and Jessie knew that when Matt saw them all having a great time he'd understand completely. No more words would be necessary and any remnant of anger would be washed away.

Between looking over the manuscript's galleys and answering Sister Maria's phone calls about plans for the picnic, Jessie was kept on a whirlwind schedule. But somehow, she and Matt found time for each other.

"It's like eating," Jessie tried to explain to Marilyn. "When you don't do it nothing else works right. That's how Matt fits into my life, Marilyn. It's crazy, it's—"

"Love," Marilyn said quietly. And before Jessie had a chance to absorb her friend's wise observation, Marilyn changed the subject.

"See these, Jess?" she asked. She held up a stack of white, printed invitations.

"Is someone getting married?"

"No. Bourke and Bailey are throwing a grand bash, at my instigation, of course. It's going to be next week at Twin Oaks Country Club, and you, young lady, will be one of the guests of honor."

"What?" Jessie took a closer look at the invitation.

"We're going to celebrate the finishing of the book. The cover art work will all be finished by then so we can show it off and we'll have bound galleys for anyone who wants to see them, which will be everyone, of course. Frederick and I felt it would be better to celebrate now when we're all so full of the book than to wait until it's off the press and we're deep in the middle of another project."

"Marilyn, that's wonderful. Except for the guest-of-honor part. I was just a peg in the wheel here, and—"

"No, dear Jess, you were far more. So shush and save your breath. You know I'll do exactly as I wish anyway."

Jessie looked down at the invitation again. She rubbed her finger over the embossed letters and smiled. So much had changed in her life over these weeks. It had all revolved around *The Manchester Rogue*, and she sincerely hoped Alexander Ridgefield was aware of how much she owed him. She looked at the huge painting of him that was enshrined in the office. He seemed to be smiling at her. Yep, she guessed he knew.

The day of the picnic dawned cool and crisp and Jessie was beside herself. The school had rented buses and she told Sister Maria she'd help hold things down to a dull roar by riding along with the kids. Marilyn was driving out in her Jaguar and Jessie assumed Matt would ride along with her. She had thought about suggesting he come on the bus so he could be with the kids, but she decided that was pushing it. Besides, he had kept his silence on the picnic, telling her the Berrys would handle everything on that end if the nuns did their part on this end and that was that. Jessie had agreed and Matt had taken her in his arms and showed her what kind of things he *did* want to pay attention to when they were together.

The first busload of kids turned into the gates of Applewood Farm at nine o'clock sharp. Jessie and Emma were on the first seat.

Emma gripped Jessie's hand. "Oh, Jessie, this is great! Will I get to ride a horse?"

Jessie looked over at her little friend. Emma was very pale today. Sister Maria had told Jessie as they boarded the bus that she needed to talk to her later. Jessie knew without asking that it was about Emma. "Well, Em, we'll see how you feel. Okay?"

Emma didn't answer because the bus doors had swung open and small bodies were piling out into the fresh air as fast as they could. Standing on the front lawn was Helen, a man Jessie supposed was her husband John and several other people she didn't know. She hurried over to Helen while the sisters and aids held the kids in check.

"Well, Helen, are you ready for this?"

Helen laughed. "We've been waiting all week for this. *Everyone* has. Come see."

Jessie followed her through the house while Helen made fast introductions. A dozen townspeople had come out to help, and Helen told her, "If I'd let everyone come who wanted to, there'd be no room for the kids." Jessie liked her husband John. He was quiet and friendly, and immediately went out to help with the kids.

"So, Jessie, what do you think?" Helen pointed to the tables lined up on the back porch and the picnic tables spread out across the back lawn.

Jessie gasped. The tables were groaning with food. There were a dozen buckets of coleslaw, huge pitchers of freshly squeezed lemonade, homemade pies of so many different kinds Jessie couldn't name them all.

"All the ingredients are homegrown," Helen said proudly. "The apples are from Applewood's trees, the gooseberries from Mr. Carey's place." She went on for five minutes listing the neighbors who had donated home-grown foods.

"I don't understand. Why, Helen?" Jessie asked.

"When they heard what was going on, they all jumped in like they were in a county fair contest. It's the first time most of them have had a chance to say thank-you to Mr. Ridgefield because he stays so remote. He doesn't allow appreciation."

Jessie nodded. "I know. He likes his privacy."

"An understatement, Jessie, if I ever heard one. The man is nearly a hermit. Or *was* before you came along. Strangest thing."

"Him being alone?"

"Oh, that's not so strange in itself. We have an number of those types around here. But if you ask me, Mr. Ridge-field's not really a loner. Not near as much as he pre-

tends, anyway. I mean, this house, it wasn't built for one."
Her son Danny pulled on her shirttail then, his smiling face
splotched with a smelly, bright yellow substance. Helen
groaned. "My little artist," she said, winking at Jessie, and
hurried off to clean up the pot of mustard the little boy had
used to fingerpaint the paper plates and himself.

Helen's words stayed with Jessie. She worked hard at
not thinking about the future, but when she was out at
Applewood the resolve was so difficult, it was almost
painful. She loved it all so—the house, the large, warm
rooms, the land and woods and creek. And she loved Matt.
Everything fit together so perfectly. And it didn't fit together at all.

"All right, Jessie, lead me to my grill."

Jessie looked up to see Marilyn standing in the doorway. She wore brand new designer jeans that fit her becoming shape perfectly. On her feet were polished leather
boots with heels so high Jessie wondered how she kept her
balance. A gorgeous forest green suede jacket completed
her outfit. She looked incredibly beautiful, straight out of
a *Vogue* magazine.

Jessie grinned. "Never in a million years have I seen a
hot-dog cook who can hold a candle to you, Marilyn
Owens. You're wonderful!" Jessie rushed over and hugged
her friend so hard she worried later that she might have left
finger marks on the expensive suede.

"I've never done anything like this before. I'm actually
looking forward to it. And look at this food!"

Jessie nodded, her eyes darting to the hallway that led
to the front of the house. "Marilyn, where's Matt? Did he
come out with you?" She started to walk toward the front
of the house.

"Matt?" Marilyn looked at her quizzically. "You didn't
expect Matt out here, did you?"

Jessie spun around. "What do you mean?"

"I mean he's not coming. At least that's what he indicated to me. I don't think he ever considered it. This isn't his kind of thing, Jessie." Her voice softened as she saw the stricken look on Jessie's face.

"But I thought—" Jessie stopped, then started over. "But it's his place. Surely he'd come if only to be sure we'd leave it in one piece."

"I think he trusts you to do that."

Jessie bit down hard on her bottom lip. Then she looked up at Marilyn with her beautiful blond hair and gorgeous clothes, ready to cook a hundred hot dogs for kids she didn't know. "You know, Marilyn, this really isn't your thing, either, but you're here."

Marilyn nodded. She could see the hurt and anger in Jessie's eyes. "Yes, I am, but you wouldn't have *expected* me to come, would you? I volunteered. Matt didn't. It's really a matter of choice."

Marilyn was right, but he could have come because of *her*, couldn't he? Jessie forked her fingers through her hair. "I suppose you're right," she said grudgingly.

"It isn't that he didn't contribute anything. Look out there."

Marilyn pointed toward the east lawn and Jessie peered out through the screens. An old-fashioned carousel, its platform filled with beautiful horses, was just starting up. Jessie could hear the faint beginnings of the piped nickelodeon music. "What—"

Helen walked in just then and saw them looking. "It's something, isn't it?"

"Where did it come from?"

"Mr. Ridgefield came out yesterday for a minute and said he was having it delivered. Said he thought some of the little ones might be afraid of the real ponies and this way no one's feelings would be hurt.''

Jessie's heart pounded.

"And he got us some little boats for the pond in case anyone wanted to go fishing or just row around. Elmer Carey from the hardware store is down there to make sure no one falls in." Before Jessie could comment, Helen was off, seeing about a volleyball net that had fallen down near the barns.

Jessie shook her head. This was too much. Marilyn came over and put an arm around her shoulder. "He's strange but he's lovable. Now, shouldn't we be doing something?" she asked, and gently shoved Jessie out the back door and into the child-cluttered yard.

The day went by in a blur. Besides several skinned knees, five lost jackets and one bloody nose, there were no calamities by late afternoon. Jessie was sitting on a wide hammock that swung gracefully from two maple trees. She was holding Helen's baby, Sarah, in her lap, with Emma next to her, pressed tightly against her side. Nearby, Marilyn stood behind a brick grill with a tall, puffy chef's hat perched on her blond hair. She wore the hat as proudly as a crown. Jessie laughed at her. "Marilyn, any four-star restaurant worth its salt would hire you on the spot."

Marilyn spiked a hot dog with practiced finesse and took it off the fire. "Who'd want it? This is the way to do things." She flashed a brilliant smile and Jessie could see she was having the time of her life.

"Want some more ice cream, Em?" She looked down at Emma's tired face. The day had exhausted the young girl, but she refused to stop. She'd ridden the ponies, with Jessie watching her like a hawk, and then had fished in the pond with Jessie at her side. Now her eyes were nearly closed, her lashes shadowing high, narrow cheekbones.

Emma shook her head. "I'm full, but that's great ice cream. Marilyn said Daisy's going to teach her how to make it."

Daisy, an enormous gray-haired woman who owned the ice-cream parlor in Evergreen, heard Emma's comment and nodded. "You betcha. I'll teach you, too, little one."

Emma grinned.

When Daisy had heard about the picnic for St. Bede's, she had insisted on bringing her whole operation out to Applewood because she thought the kids might like to see how ice cream was made. "City kids don't know things like that anymore," she'd told Jessie, and Jessie had hugged her tightly. Now Daisy was holding out a spoon of her ice cream to Sarah who was licking it delightedly.

"You know the way to a baby's heart, Daisy," Jessie said.

"Had eight of my own," the elderly woman said proudly. "I oughta."

Sarah reached out and tugged one of Emma's braids. Emma laughed, and then her eyes widened and she squealed. "I knew it, Jessie, I knew he'd come!" Before Jessie could register what was said, Emma was out of the hammock and running in her slow, uneven stride across the lawn.

Jessie stared after her, but she knew before she saw him who it was. Emma has asked for Matt earlier and had been genuinely saddened when Jessie said he wasn't coming. But he had come. Jessie got up from the hammock, the baby still in her arms, and followed Emma.

Emma surprised both Matt and Jessie by throwing her arms around him. Without thinking, Matt lifted her up in the air, her body weightless in his arms. "Hi, kid," he said gruffly, holding her at eye level, and then he lowered her carefully to the ground. He looked beyond her and saw Jessie. "And hello to you, too."

Jessie's heart was wedged up in her throat and she could only nod. Was she going to cry again? No, not at a picnic. People didn't cry at picnics unless they skinned their knees. "You came," she managed weakly.

Matt looked down at Emma and winked. "We have ourselves one observant friend here, right, Em?"

Emma beamed proudly at being included in Matt's private joke.

Matt looked at the brown-haired baby slobbering on Jessie's shoulder. "I know her. That's Sarah, right?"

Jessie nodded and Sarah stretched out her pudgy arms toward the nice voice.

Matt declined. "I can hold big kids like Emma here, but those little ones wiggle too much." He patted the baby's silky curls. "No offense, Sarah."

Emma took hold of Matt's hand possessively. "Come on, Matt, there're some hot dogs left."

Jessie fell in beside them and they walked back together to the picnic area. She didn't ask Matt why he had changed his mind, why he'd come, or what he was thinking. It was enough to love him gently like this, quietly, privately, knowing that for all his strangeness, Matt Ridgefield was as sensitive and loving as any man ever born. The trick was getting him to know it. She hugged the baby to her chest and vowed silently to give it her best shot.

Emma switched her allegiance from Jessie to Matt and for the rest of the day she clung tightly to him. Jessie was surprised but happy, and Matt was so gentle and good with Emma that she knew she didn't have to worry. When Matt was coerced into pitching for the twilight softball game— nuns against the kids—Emma sat on the bench because her legs were hurting her and she cheered him on from there.

When he sat at the edge of the group at the bonfire while Jessie led the kids in song, Emma curled up beside him and fell asleep.

"You like him, don't you, Emma?" Jessie asked later. Emma was sitting on the porch watching from a distance as the others roasted marshmallows.

Emma nodded. "I didn't at first because I was jealous."

"Jealous?"

"Yeah. You liked him so much, I could tell. And he liked you so much I didn't know where I'd fit."

"And now you know?"

"Yeah. There's always room. Being jealous just wastes time."

Jessie hugged her.

"Do you love him, Jessie?" Emma's huge eyes looked up at her. "Are you going to marry him?"

"Well, Emma, it's kind of complicated."

"Oh."

"I guess time will tell."

Emma shook her head vigorously. "Sister Maria tells us all we have is today. And it's true, Jessie."

Jessie didn't know what to say and she wondered why the wisdom of the world sometimes seemed to be given to children in a greater dose than to adults.

The picnic was over too soon for the kids but finally the weary adults managed to pile them all back into the buses. It was late and the sky was filled with a million blinking stars.

Matt stood on the front lawn with the people from the town and waved goodbye. He had told Jessie that he was staying the night and his eyes told her he wouldn't mind company. But she couldn't. Her help was needed on the bus. So with Emma at her side, she waved along with the others into the darkness. When the bus took off, she settled back to play with the memories of a day none of them would ever forget.

It was four days later when Marilyn walked into Matt's office unannounced. "Matt," she said, "we have to talk."

Matt glanced at his watch. "Sure, I have some time."

"It's about Jessie."

Matt's heart beat against his chest. "What's the matter with Jessie?"

"Everything!" She sat down in the chair beside his desk and spoke softly. "Oh, she's all right, Matt. She's not hurt, if that's what you think."

Matt breathed easier. "What's this all about then?" He lit his pipe and settled back in the worn leather chair. From the look on Marilyn's face, he'd better listen.

"Matt, I'm speaking to you as a friend, because other than Jessie, I'm probably the only close friend you have."

Matt frowned. "Marilyn—"

Marilyn waved her hand in the air. "Shh. Let me talk, Matthew. We've known each other forever, and that gives me some rights."

Matt took a long draw on his pipe and looked at her carefully. "Okay."

"I'm concerned about Jessie, and I just want to make sure you know what you're doing." Beneath the strong words, her voice was tender and caring. "I'm not being judgmental, but I've come to care deeply about Jessie, just like I do about you. And seeing her at that picnic with all those kids did something to me."

Matt nodded. Images of Jessie carrying babies and hugging kids and wiping away tears and ice cream from faces had plagued him for four days.

"She's a natural mother, Matt. She *loves* kids, and they love her back."

"I know that. I saw it, too." But hearing Marilyn put it into words was painful; it made the reality too jarring to hide in the shadows of his mind.

Marilyn stood up and walked around the desk to stand beside him. "I don't know everything that's in your heart, Matt. But I do know that you two love each other. Every day I see Jessie blossom and you become more alive with it, I see it deepen, and I wonder what's going to happen. She wants a family, Matt. A house with kids and love all over the place." She looked down at Matt sitting in the chair and she rubbed his shoulder gently.

Matt was silent. He hadn't slept much the night before. Marilyn knew him all right, but she didn't know the half of it. This love was beyond anything he'd ever felt before. She might see it, but what she saw was just the tip of the iceberg.

"I just hope you know what you're doing, Matt." She hugged him then and left. Matt barely noticed her departure. What Marilyn didn't say, but was behind every word was a warning about hurting Jessie. And that was what had kept him sleepless. The deeper his love grew, the more he couldn't bear to hurt her.

He'd known all along he wasn't right for Jessie. She needed someone like John Berry, a devoted husband, someone who knew how to be a father. Someone who wanted a family, a life of sharing. He could never be what she wanted. Look at the track record his family had. Even the Alexander Ridgefield Jessie was so crazy about could never have been labeled father or husband of the year. He'd had three wives and Matt wondered sometimes why Jessie never mentioned that. Maybe she hadn't wanted to notice. And maybe that's what she was doing with him—

overlooking things. But you could do that for just so long. Jessie deserved the best, and he loved her too much to deny her that.

Matt stood up and walked over to the casement windows. He stared out at the campus. It was cold today. Most of the leaves had fallen and a north wind was blowing them up in colorful gusts. Everyone was moving faster, he noticed absently. They were pushed by the cold, the faculty hunched over in heavy coats, the kids still in jean jackets, denying the end of fall as they rubbed their hands together.

The kids' picnic on Saturday had been just in time, he thought. Probably the last pleasant day of the year. At least that had worked out right. Matt walked slowly back to his desk and sat down, his pipe unlit and unnoticed between his lips. The cold he'd seen outside seemed to follow him. It seeped through his pores and settled down in his bones.

It would be a long winter, he thought.

Eleven

Matt's pensive behavior was hidden from Jessie by the frantic pace of the next few days. It seemed each minute there was something new to attend to—the book covers, an interview request from a trade magazine, decisions about attending book conventions. And then there was the Twin Oaks party Saturday night.

She'd made time on Thursday to go over to St. Bede's and see Emma. Sister Maria had told her after the picnic that Emma wasn't keeping food down and her glands were swollen. A million things raced through Jessie's mind. She wanted to be with Emma all the time, to do things for her, to somehow make up for what life had cheated her of. But Jessie knew that wasn't the best way, and Sister Maria, who was a loving, stabilizing force in Emma's life, made it easier by reminding her that Emma herself wanted more than anything to be normal as long as she could, to do what all the other kids did, to fool around and complain about school.

So Jessie hugged Emma and loved her and satisfied herself with being her good friend. And on Thursday they sat pressed together watching a funny movie on the lounge TV, laughing until tears came to their eyes.

When Jessie was leaving, Emma squeezed a piece of paper into her hand. Jessie opened it on the bus and read Emma's new wish: a manicure. Jessie laughed through the horrible, painful feelings she'd had when she left Emma. A manicure! She wanted to turn the bus around, wrap Emma in her arms and promise her not only a manicure but a pedicure and day of beauty at Neiman Marcus if she wanted to.

Matt came by later and she shared the story with him as soon as he walked in the door. He always listened carefully when she talked about Emma and never offered the platitudes and truisms that made Jessie so angry. Instead he was sad with her, agreed with her that life was awful sometimes, and held her and wiped away her tears when the horrible reality became overwhelming. Jessie knew it affected Matt. He had let himself be involved. He cared about Emma.

They ordered a pizza for dinner because as usual Jessie had nothing in the house to eat, and after pushing the dry crusts down the disposal, Matt sat with her on the lumpy couch and wrapped her tightly in his arms. He didn't say much and Jessie thought it was because of Emma. Later, when Jessie nodded off with her head on his shoulder and Johnny Carson bid them good-night from the television, Matt woke her up roughly. In the dim apartment light his eyes looked pale to Jessie, his lashes damp. And when he loved her, it was a ferocious kind of loving that she didn't quite understand. But she surprised herself by responding with her own desperate need, pressing her body against his as if she thought he could envelop her that way, protect her and make her a part of him that would never be shaken free.

Jessie stared into the cracked mirror that leaned against the wall next to her bed. It wasn't Jessie Esther Sager who looked back at her. It was some beautiful, sophisticated, assured woman whom she had never met before. Jessie turned slightly and lifted one shoulder. The silky, midnight-blue dress moved with her. It was the most elegant dress she had ever seen. She'd found it wrapped in an enormous box on her desk the day before and although there wasn't a note, she knew it was from Marilyn. It fit Jessie perfectly. *Too* perfectly, she'd complained to her next-door neighbor. But she was assured it was *supposed* to fit that way, and when Jessie tugged on the material to make it rise higher on her breasts, her neighbor scolded her and said she was acting like a Girl Scout instead of Jessie, the Author.

"Jessie, the Author," she now repeated, lifting her brows dramatically and fluffing her hair. "Ha! This is all a dream, it has to be."

Her mind shifted back to the day Matt Ridgefield had walked into her life. Nothing had been the same since. Had she met him a decade ago? A lifetime? It was all irrelevant, because the time before Matt didn't make sense. What was real now was the incredible, overwhelming love for him that filled her.

Matt hadn't said he loved her, not in words, but it didn't matter. Everything he did, his caring and the way he had helped with Emma, showed her far more plainly than words ever could.

A shadow across the mirror interrupted her thoughts. She turned around slowly. Matt was framed in the doorway. He wore a black tuxedo and held a single yellow rose in his hand.

Jessie's mouth dropped open. "Oh, my," she said. Her throat was tight and her whole body was reacting to the figure in front of her. "I can see I'm going to have to fight off masses of women tonight. They'll all be coveting your body."

Matt didn't smile. He didn't even hear her. He had hoped irrationally that she'd have changed overnight into someone he didn't know, someone he didn't love with this painful urgency. Someone he could separate himself from painlessly, with ease and understanding and a "let's be good friends" pat on the back. A foolish hope. His heart swelled at the sight of her. She was ravishing, and he loved her completely. If he could only get through tonight—*her* night—all right. And then tomorrow they would have to talk.

"Is that for me?" Jessie walked toward him carefully and pointed to the rose. Her dress made unfamiliar, swishing noises around her ankles.

"Oh," Matt said. He forced himself to focus on her words. "Yes."

Jessie laughed and looked down at her dress. The nervous, irrational thought that she could probably fit a whole bouquet of flowers in the revealing neckline of her dress made her laugh nervously.

But Matt didn't hear her laugh. When he spoke, his voice was so low, Jessie wouldn't have recognized it if he hadn't been standing only a foot away from her. "Jessie," he said slowly, "you're beautiful. I—"

"Shh," Jessie whispered. Her fingers touched his lips lightly. "For some peculiar reason, I feel tearful tonight, and I think it will spot my silk dress. So let's just go, okay?" She took the rose and pinned it to the lacy shawl Marilyn had loaned her, and then she let Matt help drape it across her bare shoulders. "There," she said. "My beautiful rose and I are ready. Shall we?"

Matt looked down at her smiling, lovely face and felt a part of him crumble. Then he took her arm and walked her out into the night.

"Jessie is absolutely radiant!" Marilyn exclaimed to Matt as the two of them sat at a round table and watched the swirl of Jessie's blue silk dress across the dance floor. The dinner had been superb, the speeches considerably brief, and now the party goers were flocking to the dance floor. Nearly every man in the room had wanted to dance with Jessie and she was now being held in the arms of a delighted Frederick Bourke.

"Yep, she sure is," said Matt. He motioned for a tuxedoed waiter to bring him another Scotch and water. "She's a beautiful, beautiful woman."

Marilyn frowned. "Matt, it's been some time since I've seen you inhale drinks like this."

"It's a celebration, right?" Matt said. He lifted his glass to Marilyn and smiled crookedly.

"Are you all right?" Marilyn drew her brows together and looked intently at Matt. "What's wrong?"

The music stopped and Matt watched Jessie weaving her way through the crowds. People stopped her and she spoke graciously to each, her eyes sparkling and her face radiant. He tore his eyes away and looked back at Marilyn. "Whatever's wrong, I'll make right. It's about time, don't you think?" He patted her hand, then took another drink of Scotch. His eyes sought Jessie again.

Marilyn nodded but she was concerned about Matt. He was a rock, always in control, but tonight he looked torn apart.

"We should dance," Matt said suddenly. He stood abruptly and looked down at Marilyn. "May I have the honor, Marilyn?"

Marilyn stood without speaking, puzzled at his behavior, and the two moved slowly across the room.

Jessie watched Marilyn and Matt dance from a private spot she had found next to some French doors. A huge potted plant hid her from the party goers and the respite was a welcome relief. Her heartbeat picked up as Matt unknowingly danced by her. His dark head was down, listening intently to something Marilyn was saying. He was startlingly handsome tonight. Her prince. And here she was, Cinderella at her ball.

She sought Matt out again, but this time she couldn't find him and when she moved to get a better view, she saw that he and Marilyn had returned to their table. Jessie hurried over. She'd been apart from him too long. Besides, she needed to share her exciting news with him.

"You two make a handsome couple," she said, walking up to the table and placing a hand each on their shoulders. "But now it's my turn. May I have this dance, sir?" She made a slight bow toward Matt, then lifted her lids and looked into his eyes. They were pale and tired eyes, not the eyes of her prince at all.

Matt got up from the table too fast and his highball glass turned over, sending amber liquid snaking across the linen tablecloth. Marilyn looked down at it, then up at Jessie. "Never mind," she said quickly. "You two go dance. I'll get a waiter to take care of this."

Matt led Jessie across the crowded floor.

The tension in his grip was absorbed by her skin like a blast of winter air. It must be all the hoopla, she decided quickly, shoving the uncomfortable sensations into the back of her head. Matt didn't like crowds, after all. "Matt," Jessie started, "I need to talk to you." Her news would excite him, she knew, and the pale tiredness would leave his eyes.

Matt's arm was around her waist now, but they weren't dancing. They were standing quietly among moving, elegantly dressed couples. The feelings between them were so thick and palpable that Jessie wondered briefly if others could feel and see her love for Matt.

"Okay, Jessie, sure," Matt said. He took a drink from the tray of a passing waiter and then looked around the elegant room. He spotted the door to the small library and pointed to it, the liquor splashing against the side of the glass as he moved his hand. "How about in there? Beats this dance floor." He'd listen to anything she wanted to say. Be gracious, he told himself. It was her night.

Jessie nodded. Anywhere alone with Matt would be fine. The back hall or a broom closet, she wasn't fussy.

The walnut paneled room was empty of people and warmed by a blazing fire. They headed toward it naturally and Jessie stood for a second near the hearth warming her hands.

Matt watched her, his heart squeezed tightly by the emotion that seemed about to suffocate him. She was so beautiful. The dancing flames cast shadows across her face and the light reflected from her eyes. He would never love again like this.

"Jessie," he said hoarsely.

Jessie turned quickly at the sound of his voice. It was the pain in it that frightened her.

"Let's sit." He pulled her down onto the leather couch and looked down at the fingers of her hand, playing with them carefully. "Tell me your news."

"All right," she said, "and then it's your turn. See if you can match this."

Matt swallowed hard. Why wasn't his throat working? It was closed up tighter than a drum. He nodded to Jessie.

"Bourke and Bailey have decided to do a whole series of biographies." Jessie's face lit up as she spoke and Matt found it difficult to concentrate on her words. He wanted to memorize her features and the life that flowed out of her eyes.

"Stop looking at me that way, fella," she ordered, "or I'll never get this out."

Matt forced a small smile and averted his eyes. "Okay, shoot."

"Well, Frederick told me tonight that Bourke and Bailey wants me as the chief writer on the project."

"Of the biographies?" The tone of her voice told him that this was important to her. Matt pulled his brows together to force concentration.

"Yes. And not only local people like your great-grandfather, but others—historical figures from all over. I'll even have a say in picking!"

Matt finished his drink in one swallow, then set the glass on a small end table. It thudded heavily.

"Matt?" Jessie leaned toward him. She had seen him take several drinks in rapid succession earlier and it had bothered her, but she tried to ignore it, telling herself people could drink and not turn into her father. Matt could handle himself just fine. Now she saw the cold set to his jaw and she began to shiver. "Does my news upset you?"

Matt shook his head. His voice was louder than normal. "Absolutely, positively not. I think it's great news, and I never doubted for a minute you'd make it. And the timing on all this is perfect. You'll have new responsibilities, you'll be traveling—"

Jessie pulled her brows together until her forehead began to ache. He wasn't making sense. It must be the liquor. "No, not really. There might be some travel but I'm settling in right here." She forced a laugh. "Jess, the homing pigeon, that's me."

"Well, whatever," Matt said, waving one hand through the air. "The point is, a new life is starting for you and I think you ought to take advantage of it. Move ahead full steam."

Jessie took his face between her palms. "Matt, what is the matter?"

Matt removed her hands and held them for a moment in his lap. Maybe it was meant to be now. The pain inside him squeezed logic away. Now or never, but how was he going to let her go? "Jessie, I'm beating around the bush. What I need to say is that this is a good time for us to break it off—"

"Matt!" The single word came out in a gasp.

"Wait, Jess, and hear me out. We both knew we couldn't go on *ad infinitum*. You've got a career beginning, and you need to start looking for a husband, and—"

"Stop it! What are you saying to me?"

Matt touched her, then took his hand away quickly. "You need someone who can build a family with you, Jess. That's what you've always wanted."

"But I thought—" Her voice choked and the words wouldn't come. She tried again. "I thought things were different now. I thought maybe—"

Matt stopped her. "Jess," he said slowly, "I've never deceived you. I never pretended to be anything other than what I am." Sadness coated his words.

Jessie stared into the fire and felt everything inside her shrivel up into a hard, small knot. And then, in a sweep, all the hollows were filled with an anger that nearly blinded her. She looked at Matt.

"You *didn't* deceive me? Oh, but that's where you're dead wrong, Professor Ridgefield." Jessie stood and stared down at him. "Every time you loved me, you claimed to be something else."

Her voice broke and the sting of tears caused the colors in the room to run together. She couldn't see Matt anymore; the man she loved was nothing but a colorless shape on the sofa. With the back of her hand she wiped away the tears. "You know what you are, Matt? You're a selfish man. You've used your mother's death and your father's suicide as an excuse. They failed you, so you'll never take a chance, never put yourself out to love another person, never take on the responsibility of filling another's life. Do you know what that is, Matt?" The tears were running freely now, down her cheeks and falling onto her dress.

Matt sat still. Her anger was settling into his loss. But maybe it's better this way, he thought. Maybe anger will make it easier. He wished he had that crutch. All he felt was a numbing, suffocating sadness.

"That, Matt," Jessie said, her words coming in painful gasps, "is a terrible cop-out on life."

She walked over to the door, then looked back at the figure silhouetted by the firelight. His dark head was down, supported by his hands. He didn't look at her. A terrible, frightening emptiness filled her. "Goodbye, Matt," she said quietly, and walked slowly out of the room.

Some days she almost hated him for causing her this horrible, unyielding pain. It was permanently attached to her, an iron chain fastened tightly around her heart. The anger and terror and love all melded together into an unbearable weight. Jessie felt as if she were going to die.

"He did it for you, Jessie," Marilyn said for the hundredth time that week. She had insisted Jessie come over for dinner and they sat together over the cook's untouched Poulet Flamand.

"I can't buy it. He did it for *him*, so he wouldn't have to give any of himself away."

Marilyn shook his head. "That's your anger speaking. You know as well as I that Matt's tragedy handicapped him."

Jessie nodded and the slight movement caused the tears to begin again. They flowed down her cheeks and onto her lap. She wondered absently if her cheeks were carved yet from the tears that seemed to have no end.

Marilyn shoved a box of Kleenex in front of her.

Jessie looked up so sorrowfully that Marilyn had to look away. "Marilyn," she asked, her voice choked with tears, "do you think we can work this out? Do you think he'll come back?"

"Only if he thinks he can give you what you need, hon. That's how much he loves you."

Jessie blew her nose noisily. "I don't know what to do. I love him so much. Maybe I'm the one who needs to make an adjustment."

"No, Jess. Your love for him would be crippled if you did that."

"But I don't think I can handle this. I can't be without him. I can't—"

Marilyn hugged her tightly and noticed the boney feeling to her shoulders. She forced a stern, authoritarian tone into her voice. "You need sleep and food, or you'll be of no use to anyone. And there *are* other people who need you, you know."

The harsh ring of the phone stopped Jessie's tears long enough for her to take the receiver when Marilyn handed it to her. "It's Sister Maria," she whispered.

Calls from St. Bede's frightened her now. She spent some time each day with Emma, who had good days and bad days. When she was feeling all right, Jessie would bundle her up until she looked like an Eskimo, her thin face nearly hidden in the folds of scarf, and they would walk slowly along the grounds of St. Bede's. Emma talked a lot about winter and ice skating, about sleigh rides and building snowmen, as if making plans would bring about more days and more life. Jessie listened to her and loved her, and then went home and discovered there were still more tears, even when she thought she was dry.

"Hello, Sister," Jessie said. She forced a cheerfulness into her voice. That was *her* trick—if she was cheerful, the news wouldn't be bad.

But it wasn't Sister Maria; it was Emma whose voice came over the phone line. "I just wanted to know if you were coming to see me tomorrow," Emma said. "We tracked you down." Her small voice was hoarse, but she sounded happy.

"Well, I can see that. How did you find me?"

"Oh." She paused mysteriously. Then she said matter-of-factly, "Matt."

"Matt?"

Emma sounded pleased with herself. "Yes. When he was here tonight, he said you might be at Miss Owens's if you weren't home and he gave us the phone number. Sister thought we might be bothering you, but I said no, that you said I could always call."

"Of course you can, sweetie. You're absolutely right." Matt had been there? The emotion swirled and burned in her stomach. He'd been to see Emma?

"So are you coming?"

Jessie pulled her thoughts together so she could listen to Emma. "Coming? Of course I am. Wild horses couldn't keep me away."

"Okay, good. I love you, Jessie," Emma said, and she hung up the phone.

* * *

Jessie stopped at the market and filled a basket with fresh fruit to take to Emma. She tried to think of things that would tempt her friend to eat, even though she knew Emma was probably passing most of it along to the other kids.

Jessie walked down the wide, clean hall to Emma's room. She hoped Emma didn't ask about Matt today. She had kept after Jessie so relentlessly after the Twin Oaks party that she finally had to explain that she and Matt didn't see each other anymore. Jessie worried about upsetting Emma, but Sister Maria told Jessie later that Emma knew anyway, that sometimes children had special sensors that picked up things adults missed entirely.

When Jessie reached Emma's doorway, she spotted her sitting on her window seat opening a large, flat box in her lap. She looked good today, Jessie decided. "Hi, sweetie," she said, and as the words moved across the room, she saw him.

He had been sitting near the bookcase watching Emma, and she had missed him at first. But at the sound of her voice he turned around quickly.

"Hi, Jessie," Emma greeted her cheerfully. "Matt's here."

The blue of his eyes was as deep as ever, but beneath it were dark hollows that made him look older. "Hello, Matt," Jessie said, forcing a smile and wondering how long it would be before she could breathe again.

"I didn't know you were coming," Matt told her. "I'm sorry."

He looked as sad as she felt, Jessie thought. What a waste. And then she glanced quickly at Emma. Emma was still fussing with the box, her eyes downcast and her lips curved in a smile. She'd planned this. Her sensitive Emma had invited them both to come, had tried to play peacemaker. The thought brought unexpected tears to Jessie's eyes and she fought against them fiercely until the sting eased and her vision cleared.

Emma finally pulled her gift from the tissues in the box. It was a large framed photograph of Applewood Farm. Her small, strained voice was alive with pleasure. "Thank you so much. I knew you'd do it, Matt, thank you."

"A man in Evergreen took it. He has a shop filled with pictures of the country. We'll go out and see it some day and maybe find another one you like."

Emma nodded and Jessie fought a new surge of tears.

"But now," Matt was saying in the distance. "I have to leave. I want to see Sister Maria for a minute. You two visit."

He hugged Emma and headed for the door. He paused just for a second, touched Jessie lightly on the arm and was gone.

Jessie smiled with forced brightness. She told Emma she'd go get some sodas, then hurried into the bathroom down the hall to hide the new tears in a cold-tiled stall.

The weekend was cold and rainy and Jessie thought any minute it would turn to snow. But it didn't, and she decided it was probably her fault. The feelings inside of her were so gray and dismal that they spread to the outside world.

On Monday Sister Maria called and asked to see her, assuring her Emma was fine. Better, in fact, than she'd been in days.

Jessie sat in the straight-backed chair in the director's office and couldn't hold in the gasp of total astonishment when Sister Maria explained the reason for the meeting. "I don't understand," she finally managed to say. She needed to have it explained one more time.

"Apparently Professor Ridgefield heard about Emma's wish trip that you two talked about."

"It was a kind of dream, something that would keep her thinking ahead."

"Yes, I understand." Sister Maria folded her hands on the top of her desk and smiled kindly at Jessie. "Well, Professor Ridgefield, Emma's doctor and I talked the other day while you were with Emma and we think it would be possible for her to go on a short trip—two days at the most—and that it would be the most wonderful medicine in the world for her. Professor Ridgefield has made all the arrangements. All we need is for you to say you will take our Emma, and everything will be set."

"Sister, I can't believe this."

"Nor I, Jessie. But the professor seems to have a soft spot in his heart for Emma, and I think he rather likes you, as well."

"When can we go?"

"The doctor says as soon as possible. According to the professor, plans could be set for this weekend if it's agreeable to you."

Jessie couldn't believe what she was hearing. Emma's wish trip. She closed her eyes for a second to let it seep in, but all rational thought was blocked out by a myriad of emotions too strong to deal with. "Is...is Matt going along?" Jessie finally asked.

"No. But he has set everything up so your accommodations will be as comfortable as possible. Everything will be taken care of."

Comfortable didn't begin to describe Emma's dream trip. The joy that filled her frail body was so buoyant that Jessie thought they could probably get to Boston fine without use of the first-class airline tickets. But they used them anyway, and when they arrived at the airport and were met by a uniformed chauffeur who led them to a stretch limo with a television, Jessie thought Emma was going to do cartwheels on the leather seats. They toasted one another with sparkling apple juice from the bar, and Emma sighed and leaned her head back against the cushion. "Jessie, am I dreaming?"

"If you are, darling," Jessie said, "we're dreaming together. We're on the same cloud."

"Do you think Matt is Santa Claus?" Emma asked.

"Well, I think for sure he's amazing," Jessie whispered.

When the limousine pulled up beneath the canopy of their hotel, the friendly driver informed them he would be at their service around the clock until he took them back to the airport the next day. All they had to do was call the desk and the car would be waiting. Then he saluted Emma jovially and helped her out of the car.

The weekend went by in a blur and Jessie was grateful there wasn't any time to think. Matt had outdone himself, and she forced herself to concentrate on the flurry of events and not the man responsible for them.

By the time Emma and Jessie had to return home, they had acquired a carload of gifts, been chauffeured all over the city at dusk, dined at the city's finest restaurants, been entertained at the theater and had watched the lights flicker over Charles River as they drank tea with honey.

Sleep didn't come easily for Jessie those two nights. Matt had been with her and Emma the whole weekend. Everything they'd done, every sight they'd seen, he'd been there. And he'd been wrapped up in her dreams at night. A part of her.

Emma slept nearly the whole flight home and when she awoke at the grinding sound of the landing gear, Jessie noticed her cheeks were pink and her eyes were filled with happiness. "Well, Em, we're home," she said.

"Jessie, it was perfect. Our perfect trip. I'm sad it's over."

"But it's not over, Em." Jessie took Emma's hand and pressed it to her heart, then to her own. "It's here. And it'll stay there forever, ready for us to pull out whenever we want."

Emma nodded happily. "I have one more wish—"

"*Another* wish?"

"Yep. I don't know whether to give it to you or to Matt."

"Well, I don't know, either," Jessie said. She half listened, her mind running ahead to the problems of getting their bags and finding a cab on a busy Sunday night. Emma was still tired, she could tell, and Jessie was anxious to get her back to St. Bede's.

"I think, Matt," Emma said finally.

"He's a better bet, huh?" Jessie said. She stood and pulled their coats from the overhead compartment.

"We'll see," Emma said mysteriously.

When they walked inside the terminal and found another uniformed chauffeur, with Sister Maria standing beside him waving, and then were told that Matt had a cab driver lined up to deliver the bags and boxes later that night so they wouldn't have to wait, Jessie decided Emma was right. Matt was a sure bet.

And no matter what reason dictated, there was no way she was going to live whatever life she had left without him. *Somehow* she'd figure this out.

Twelve

Jessie wandered around the grounds of the campus for two hours, her hands stuffed in the deep pockets of her coat to keep them warm. But she barely felt the harsh winds that picked up pieces of bark and dead leaves and whipped them around her ankles. "Okay," she said out loud. "You're a half person without Matt Ridgefield, Jessica Esther. How do you handle that?" She kicked a lost tennis ball into a pile of leaves. "The love's there. You didn't choose it, it just *is*. So you make the best of it. Right? And whether he knows it or not, he has to do the same. Concessions, that's the name of the game."

A student walking along the narrow path and reading a textbook looked up at her curiously.

Jessie stared at him. "Don't think all the answers are in books, sonny, because they're not!" She spoke with such urgency that the man was startled and stumbled over a root, dropping his book.

"Right," muttered the student as he knelt on the ground to pick it up.

Jessie stopped for a minute, watching him but not seeing anything. Her body was as still as a statue and her mind raced crazily. Then she turned like a British guard changing shifts and faced Matt's building.

"Okay, Sager, this is it," she said. "Give it your best shot." Her heart wobbled. A tiny fear remained and it was enough to crumble her on a second's notice. She couldn't think about, couldn't even touch on the possibility that he really didn't want to share his life with her.

Jessie took off, the tail of her coat catching the breeze and flapping behind her. The student, left kneeling on the cold ground, wondered why they let nuts like Jessie on campus.

She walked into Matt's office. "I came to see Matt," Jessie told Dena.

"Oh, Jessie, I'm so sorry. He left about an hour ago."

Jessie's heart fell to her feet. "Do you . . . do you know where he went?"

"Well, as a matter of fact, I do. He got a call from his little friend at St. Bede's and he went right on over there."

"St. Bede's." Jessie didn't realize she had spoken out loud until Dena answered.

"Yes. He's attached to a little girl over there." Dena paused for a minute, then started talking again. "I know it's not my place, Jessie, but something's wrong with the professor. He hasn't been himself for days now. The only time he smiles is when he talks to that little girl and all the rest of the time he paces."

She waited for Jessie to respond but Jessie could feel the emotion swelling up in her again. She knew the symptoms by now and knew how long she had before the tears came. "Is he coming back here?" she managed to ask quietly.

Dena shrugged. "I don't know. He's usually so good about telling me but these past days he doesn't even do that."

"Okay, Dena, thanks," Jessie said, and she hurried out the door.

The bus was pulling away from the curb when Jessie dashed around the corner of Oak Street. "Oh, please, stop!" she yelled. The desperation in her voice caused a passerby to motion the driver to hold up for a minute.

Jessie collapsed on the front seat and wondered how long her luck would hold out. It seemed to be wearing thin. An omen? No, she wouldn't allow those thoughts. She calmed herself down and was breathing normally when the bus stopped half a block from St. Bede's and let her off.

But her breath stopped completely when Sister Maria told her Matt had left a half hour earlier. Jessie slumped down in the chair near the nun's desk. "Do you know where he went?"

"No, dear, I don't know. But he looked most cheerful when he left. Emma must have cheered him up."

Jessie smiled in spite of the painful void that was opening again inside her. "How is Em today? I'll run down to see her in a second."

Sister Maria was silent.

The silence was disturbing. Jessie looked up. "Sister?"

"Emma doesn't want to go back to the hospital so I think she pretends sometimes. But she still has the fever that started yesterday and eating is becoming a chore. The doctor is concerned. She's not getting better, Jessie."

Jessie felt numb. She nodded.

"You go see her, though, because she has a mischievous sparkle in her eyes that defies what I'm telling you. You'll see."

Jessie hurried down to Emma's room. Emma was lying on the bed, her warm-up clad, thin leg sticking out from beneath a plaid blanket. Her eyes were closed.

Jessie tiptoed in and kissed her gently on the forehead. "I love you, Em."

"I know," Emma whispered hoarsely. Her lids opened, followed by a slow smile.

Jessie slid down on the bed. "How're you doing?"

"I gave Matt my wish today."

"Did he make it come true?"

"How are you, Jessie?"

"Emma, are you changing the subject?"

Emma nodded and Jessie saw the sparkle Sister was talking about. It flickered in her huge eyes.

"Want me to read you a book?" Jessie asked.

"No," Emma said. "I think you should leave now."

Jessie wrinkled her forehead. "Emma—"

"I'm tired."

Jessie stared at the little girl for a minute. The small smile was still there at the edges of her mouth. "Where's Matt, Emma?"

Emma shrugged her thin shoulder. "I dunno. But I suppose if I were Matt and I needed to work things out I'd go where I could think best. And I suppose if I were you I'd go find him. 'Night, Jessie." Emma began to cough and then she rolled over and pulled the blanket up to her ears.

Jessie sat there for a minute looking at her. Then she kissed her again, tucking the blanket beneath Emma's bony hip and headed for the telephone in the lounge.

He wasn't at the office or his condominium. Jessie nibbled on her bottom lip. "Of course," she said out loud.

Sister Maria walked by. "Did you say something, Jessie?"

"Yes, Sister. Do you have a car?"

* * *

Matt turned the corner and drove away from Jessie's apartment. His heart was full and his hands smelled like oysters.

Weeks ago his thoughts had been right—Jessie was a part of him. She'd done something to him, and there wasn't any way he could live the rest of his life without her.

He thought of little Emma who had also won her way into his heart, and he could still feel the bright smile she'd had for him today. Less than two months ago he didn't think himself capable of loving anyone in a lasting, committed way, and now there were two females who had stolen his heart and for whom he'd move heaven and earth if he could.

A car pulled up beside him at the stoplight and he glanced over at the driver. His heart stopped, and then slowly he began to breath again. It had looked like Jessie for a minute. *His* Jessie. But it wasn't.

He thought back over the days without her. Wasted days. "Just let me have right now," Emma had said a few days ago when he was helping her into her bed. She'd muttered it softly, not meaning for him to hear. So little time. So much time wasted. Matt pushed his foot on the gas and turned into the empty country road.

He had thought all night about how to talk to Jessie. He'd hurt her badly, he knew. But whatever the hurt, he'd have to explain it away, love it away. Somehow he had to get Jessie to give him another chance. He needed her so desperately he couldn't think, couldn't function. The clerk in James Fish Market had actually had to count his money out for him when he'd bought the oysters. And Jessie's landlord had looked at him skeptically when she found him prowling outside her door. It was only her nosiness that had saved Matt. She'd seen him with Jessie from her window each time he'd brought her home, so she finally allowed him in. She followed close behind him all the while and scowled severely while he carefully placed the plate of delicate oysters in the refrigerator.

"Those smell awful bad," she'd complained, and Matt had agreed, promising to have the whole apartment cleaned and scrubbed the next day.

Promises ... he'd made so many in his mind. He'd be good to Jessie, he'd make up for every minute wasted. And he knew he could. It had amazed him when the realization struck that the love she'd planted in him had added all sorts of dimensions to his life, given him new dreams, new hopes. And together— The thought caught in his mind and grew until he almost missed the turn to Applewood Farm. *Together.* It had to be. There had to be a together.

There were lots of reasons Matt could have gone out to Applewood Farm midday on a Tuesday, Jessie told herself. She didn't doubt that's where he was. And Emma probably knew it all along. Jessie jiggled the unfamiliar gearshift on the nun's car. He could be locking out the world, locking out *her*. She had no reason to think otherwise; that's what the farm had meant to him before, hadn't it?

He could have gone out there to think things through, in which case she'd be barging in and unwelcome.

Or he could have gone out there to...to what? There was a third reason, she felt, but she couldn't for the life of her put her finger on what it was. If he wanted to come and tell Jessie he loved her and couldn't live without her, the farm wasn't the place to go. The car lurched as she switched into fourth gear. Why didn't they build one kind of car that everyone could drive and leave it at that?

The journey seemed to last forever and yet was over in a second. Suddenly Jessie was driving through the familiar gates of Applewood Farm, her heart in her throat along with her carefully rehearsed words. Lights flickered on in the house.

Jessie thought she was going to faint.

Slowly she walked up to the front door, but it opened before she could lift her hand to knock. Matt stood there, the firelight behind him showing off the wonderful contours of his body. His face was hidden in shadows. Jessie's mouth opened to speak, but before she could form words, her eyes filled with huge, hot tears that rolled down her cheeks.

"Come here," Matt said roughly, and pulled her into the curve of his arms. Matt pushed the door closed and they stood there in the hall, his arms holding her tightly, her head pressed into his chest, and her tears soaking his plaid shirt.

Finally Jessie pulled away and fumbled for a Kleenex in her pocket.

"You found the oysters?" Matt asked. He ran his hand down her backbone. It was hard to allow any space between them. He felt himself fighting for every ounce of restraint.

"Oysters?" Jessie echoed, her voice cracking at the end.

"In your refrigerator."

Jessie wiped her eyes. "Matt, maybe we need to start over." Jessie forced a smile on her face. He had held her and she had felt the love in his arms. It was there and it was real, no matter what else happened.

"Okay," he said. "Start over, wherever you want, but it'll end the same way. I'll love you just as completely, Jess."

"You will?" The words were spoken with a croak. And were followed by a new torrent of tears.

"Forever." He kissed away a tear. Then he pulled her over to the couch and pulled her tightly against him. "You're everything to me, Jess, my whole life—"

"No, hush, it's my turn." She pressed her fingers against his lips. She tried twice to talk, then finally managed to find some words. "I love you, Matt. I came to tell you that. I know we have things to work out, but I can't handle my life without you. You're so much a part of me, a part of my happiness, my dreams, my hopes." She ignored the tears now. "I'll make concessions, if only you'll say we can work this out. And I know, no matter what you say, that we can figure it out."

Matt rubbed his cheek against her hair. The days without Jessie had been torture, and touching her now was making him crazy. But he knew it needed to be taken slowly so the earlier hurt and anger could be washed away completely and not be a part of this night. "You're right. You're right about a lot of things. I love you. I knew it a long time ago, but I didn't know what it meant until I was without you. What I hadn't anticipated was what your love did for me. It changed some parts of me around."

"Not all of them, I hope."

Matt laughed and it separated the thick emotion into more manageable strands. "My same, wonderful Jess," he said and kissed the tip of her nose.

"I know what you mean. I've changed, too. I don't think I paid much attention, before, to the fact that everyone doesn't think like I do, or approach life like I do, and I need to allow for that. I railroaded you into doing things."

"And sometimes that's not good, but you were right about some things, and it's taken me far too long to realize it. I *was* hiding, I was copping out. I was madder than hell at you for a while, but you were right. I've lost too many years, Jess, I'm not going to lose any more. I look at Emma and I feel shame that I've been such a selfish fool."

Jessie tilted her head back and kissed him. "No, that's too harsh. But Emma has taught me a few things, too."

Matt nuzzled her neck. "How much do we have to figure out before I can show you how much I've missed you?"

"Just a little more, love. We have to figure out why you have two champagne glasses on the coffee table and a bottle chilling over there. It almost looks as if you were expecting someone."

"The oysters," Matt murmured. "The note with the oysters."

"I know I've been a little crazy these past days, but Matt, I think you may have lost it. I don't know what you're talking about."

"You didn't find the oysters in your refrigerator?"

She shook her head.

"They're there. Waiting for you. Emma and I figured it out. It all started with her wish."

"She told me she gave it to you."

"And I told her it was as good as done, that I'd had the same wish for some days. We just needed to convince you."

"A three-way wish?"

"Yep. So Emma and I came up with a little game to lure you out here. The oysters were for old times' sake, but the note next to the lemon talked about swearing at bagels. It all rhymed, of course."

Jessie nodded, her throat feeling tight.

"And taped on the window of the bagel store was a note about a certain picture of my great-grandfather."

"In my office."

"And on the picture of the mayor in your office was talk of a rendezvous point—the house a little girl dreamed of a long, long time ago."

Jessie shifted on the couch and her arms curled around his neck. "Have I said how much I love you?"

He nodded. "Now's proving time. Will you marry me?"

Jessie was quiet for a few seconds. "Do you really want that, Matt?"

"That's one thing you should know about me, Jess. I never say things I don't mean. Sometimes it takes me a while to say them, but I mean them when I do. Besides, there's Emma's wish. That's no small matter, you know." He reached in his pocket and pulled out a crumpled piece of paper. He smoothed it on his knee, then held it up for Jessie to read. Written in Emma's neat handwriting were the words:

One more wish:
To be a bridesmaid

                                              Love
                                              Emma

Matt wiped away the beginning of the new batch of tears that moved slowly down Jessie's cheeks.

"It'll have to be soon, Jess, but I think we can do it. I think Emma can do it. She's tough and she wants this awfully bad. We can have it at home, out here. In front of the fire. The nuns can come. A few friends."

"You're something else, Professor Ridgefield." Just when she thought she was drained of emotion, a new wave swept through her. She pressed tight against him.

"Are we through talking?" Jessie asked, her body straining toward him.

"Just one more thing."

"Promise?"

"Yep."

Jessie's fingers massaged his chest. "Okay."

"I want a child before I'm forty."

Jessie's voice caught. Her heart was so full she wondered if it was dangerous. Did hearts ever fill too fully? "When's your birthday?" she asked. Her voice was thick with tears and love.

"September."

"We'd better get busy."

"That's what I thought, too."

Matt's arms went around her then, and talk didn't matter anymore.

*   *   *   *   *

⚛. SILHOUETTE®

Desire®

ANOTHER BRIDE FOR A BRANIGAN BROTHER!

Branigan's Touch
by Leslie Davis Guccione

Available in October 1989

You've written in asking for more about the Branigan brothers, so we decided to give you Jody's story—from *his* perspective.

Look for Mr. October—*Branigan's Touch*—a *Man of the Month*, coming from Silhouette Desire.

Following #311 *Bittersweet Harvest*, #353 *Still Waters* and #376 *Something in Common*, *Branigan's Touch* still stands on its own. You'll enjoy the warmth and charm of the Branigan clan—and watch the sparks fly when another Branigan man meets his match with an O'Connor woman!

SD523-1

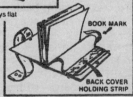

Silhouette Romance®

JOIN TOP-SELLING AUTHOR
EMILIE RICHARDS
FOR A SPECIAL ANNIVERSARY

Only in September, and only in Silhouette Romance, we'll be bringing you Emilie's twentieth Silhouette novel, *Island Glory* (SR #675).

Island Glory brings back Glory Kalia, who made her first—and very memorable—appearance in *Aloha Always* (SR #520). Now she's here with a story—and a hero—of her own. Thrill to warm tropical nights with Glory and Jared Farrell, a man who doesn't want to give any woman his heart but quickly learns that, with Glory, he has no choice.

Join Silhouette Romance now and experience a taste of *Island Glory*.

 # $Silhouette\ Desire$ ®

COMING
NEXT MONTH

#523 BRANIGAN'S TOUCH—Leslie Davis Guccione
October's *Man of the Month*, Jody Branigan, couldn't help it if
Megan O'Connor disapproved of the notorious Branigan brood. So
how did *he* get talked into charming the beguiling redhead?

#524 WITH A LITTLE SPICE—Sara Chance
When Ginger Bellwood realized she'd been manipulated into falling
for Michael Sheridan, she was hurt and disillusioned. But then
Michael risked all to give her the truth . . . and his love.

#525 A PACKAGE DEAL—Ariel Berk
After raising six younger siblings, Heather Baldwin knew she wasn't
cut out for motherhood. So handsome Douglas Baldwin seemed
perfect—except for one small detail: he had a son.

#526 BEFORE DAWN—Terry Lawrence
Art therapist Annie Rosetti was determined to help blond, brawny
Cliff Sullivan learn to deal with his temporary blindness. But when
his sight was restored, would he still need Annie?

#527 ADDED DELIGHT—Mary Lynn Baxter
Widower Joshua Malone had hired Melissa Banning to keep his house
and his children. But Melissa knew she'd be happy only if she could
keep his heart, as well.

#528 HIS GIRL FRIDAY—Diana Palmer
Danetta Marist was in a quandary. Her gruff, handsome boss set her
heart on fire, but if she got too close to Cabe Ritter, would she be
forever burned?

AVAILABLE NOW:

Desire

EXTRACURRICULAR ACTIVITY

When Jessie Sager impulsively told a
stranger she'd lost her job, she never
expected him to offer to help. Matt
Ridgefield explained he was used to finding
work for his students — but he looked more
like a rugged cowboy than a Connecticut
professor. And while his "big brother"
intentions were nice, desire soon made
a simple friendship impossible.

Matt was haunted by a tragic past and
sought peace in a solitary existence. But
Jessie's carefree style — and sweet
sensuality — had him questioning those
lonely nights spent in his study. She had
invaded his turf and brought her feminine
touch into his home. She was teaching him
a lesson in love . . . but could he learn to take
a chance on forever?

ISBN 0-373-05520-X

05520

0 65373 00250 1

PRINTED IN U.S.A.